"Remove your hand this instant!"

Pippa commanded.

"Nah, they'd suspect something. It's more convincing if I just tighten it around your shoulder," Luke replied.

"I'm warning you—"

"And then draw you closer to me—like this...."

"You let me go this instant—*Luke!*"

He mustn't kiss her, because if he did, her heart would melt and she would forget why she was mad at him. And she wanted to stay mad. That was always safest with Luke.

"You can't kiss me in the middle of an amusement park."

"Why not?" Luke asked plaintively.

She gave up arguing. The feeling that was spreading through her was taking over, silencing her. It was sheer happiness, of a kind she'd almost forgotten: the happiness of being with this one man, in his arms, with nothing else to worry about.

At least for a brief time.

Dear Reader,

Fall is upon us, and there's no better way to treat yourself to hours of autumn pleasure than by reading your way through these riveting romances in September's Special Edition books!

The lives and loves of the Bravo family continue with *The M.D. She* Had *To Marry,* in Christine Rimmer's popular CONVENIENTLY YOURS miniseries. In the page-turner *Father Most Wanted*, beloved writer Marie Ferrarella combines a witness protection program, a single dad with three daughters and an unsuspecting heroine to tell a love story you won't be able to put down. Bestselling author Peggy Webb deals with family matters of a different kind with yet another compelling Native American hero story. In *Gray Wolf's Woman* a loner finds the hearth and home he'd never realized he'd yearned for.

Lucy Gordon's poignant reunion romance, *For His Little Girl,* will sweep you away as an unexpected turn of events promises to reunite a family that was always meant to be. Janis Reams Hudson continues her Western family saga miniseries, WILDERS OF WYATT COUNTY, with *A Child on the Way,* a compelling amnesia story about a pregnant woman who ends up in the arms of another irresistible Wilder man. And Patricia McLinn's Wyoming miniseries, A PLACE CALLED HOME, continues with *At the Heart's Command,* a tale of a military hero who finally marches to the beat of his own heart as he woos his secret love.

We hope this month brings you many treasured moments of promise, hope and happy endings as Special Edition continues to celebrate Silhouette's yearlong 20th Anniversary!

All the best,

Karen Taylor Richman
Senior Editor

Please address questions and book requests to:
Silhouette Reader Service
U.S.: 3010 Walden Ave., P.O. Box 1325, Buffalo, NY 14269
Canadian: P.O. Box 609, Fort Erie, Ont. L2A 5X3

LUCY GORDON
FOR HIS LITTLE GIRL

Published by Silhouette Books

America's Publisher of Contemporary Romance

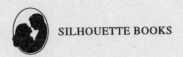 SILHOUETTE BOOKS

ISBN 0-373-24348-0

FOR HIS LITTLE GIRL

Copyright © 2000 by Lucy Gordon

This edition published by arrangement with Harlequin Books S.A.

® and TM are trademarks of Harlequin Books S.A., used under license. Trademarks indicated with ® are registered in the United States Patent and Trademark Office, the Canadian Trade Marks Office and in other countries.

Visit Silhouette at www.eHarlequin.com

Printed in U.S.A.

LUCY GORDON

met her husband-to-be in Venice, fell in love the first evening and got engaged two days later. They're still happily married and now live in England with their three dogs. For twelve years Lucy was a writer for an English women's magazine. She interviewed many of the world's most interesting men, including Warren Beatty, Richard Chamberlain, Sir Roger Moore, Sir Alec Guiness and Sir John Gielgud.

In 1985 she won the *Romantic Times* Reviewers' Choice Award for Outstanding Series Romance Author. She has also won a Golden Leaf Award from the New Jersey Chapter of RWA, was a finalist in the RWA Golden Medallion contest in 1988 and won the 1990 RITA Award in the Best Traditional Romance category for *Song of the Lorelei*.

IT'S OUR 20th ANNIVERSARY!
We'll be celebrating all year,
Continuing with these fabulous titles,
On sale in September 2000.

Intimate Moments

#1027 Night Shield
Nora Roberts

#1028 Night of No Return
Eileen Wilks

#1029 Cinderella for a Night
Susan Mallery

#1030 I'll Be Seeing You
Beverly Bird

#1031 Bluer Than Velvet
Mary McBride

#1032 The Temptation of Sean MacNeill
Virginia Kantra

Special Edition

#1345 The M.D. She *Had* To Marry
Christine Rimmer

#1346 Father Most Wanted
Marie Ferrarella

#1347 Gray Wolf's Woman
Peggy Webb

#1348 For His Little Girl
Lucy Gordon

#1349 A Child on the Way
Janis Reams Hudson

#1350 At the Heart's Command
Patricia McLinn

Desire

#1315 Slow Waltz Across Texas
Peggy Moreland

#1316 Rock Solid
Jennifer Greene

#1317 The Next Santini Bride
Maureen Child

#1318 Mail-Order Cinderella
Kathryn Jensen

#1319 Lady with a Past
Ryanne Corey

#1320 Doctor for Keeps
Kristi Gold

Romance

#1468 His Expectant Neighbor
Susan Meier

#1469 Marrying Maddy
Kasey Michaels

#1470 Daddy in Dress Blues
Cathie Linz

#1471 The Princess's Proposal
Valerie Parv

#1472 A Gleam in His Eye
Terry Essig

#1473 The Librarian's Secret Wish
Carol Grace

Chapter One

Luke had chosen his bedroom because it overlooked the golden California coast, glittering water and Manhattan Beach pier. In fact he'd bought his house on the Strand because it had this glorious view, and his first sight of it each morning was precious.

Today, as on every day, he slipped naked out of bed and went to the window. He was about to pull up the blinds when he stopped and cast a fond glance behind him to where he could see a riot of blond curls spilling across the pillow.

Dominique was a darling, but never at her best in the morning. And after the crazy night they'd had together, she deserved her sleep. Her "beauty sleep" she called it, though why the most incredible face and body in the whole of Los Angeles—no, make that the world, he thought generously—should need beauty sleep was beyond him.

He left the blind in place, pulled on some swimming shorts and went downstairs to his oversize kitchen. From his refrigerator he took out the glass of orange juice he'd squeezed the night before as he always did. He drank it slowly, savoring each mouthful of the cold, tangy liquid. He never insulted good food by hurrying it.

When he'd finished it he raced across the Strand, just as he was, and down the beach. The sting of the fresh water drove away the last of his sleep, making him ready for the new day in a life that was good in every way.

Luke Danton, thirty-four, popular, handsome, successful. For as long as he could remember, whenever he'd held out his hands, life's pleasures had fallen into them. Not without effort on his part, for he was a man who worked as hard as he played, which was very hard. But his efforts almost always brought their just rewards.

For an hour he bodysurfed, challenging the waves and enjoying the sense that they were challenging him back. At last he turned and stood, looking back at the panorama of the beach and the houses beyond, fixing his eyes lovingly on his own home, his pride and joy. The price had made him gulp, but it was worth every cent.

As a child he'd played on this beach. As a youth he would bum around it until his mother screamed at him. But in the intervals between screaming she'd taught him to cook, and he'd found his true vocation. As a man he'd returned to buy a house just a couple of blocks away from the Manhattan Pier.

He hurried home to take a shower. Dominique was still asleep, so he closed the bathroom door before bursting into tuneless song under the stream of water.

There wasn't an ounce of fat on his lean, hard body, but he never bothered with workouts. His crazy energy, demon-hard work and hours in the sea kept him in shape. His legs were long and muscular, his hips taut, his shoulders broad.

His face looked younger than his thirty-four years, with a permanent touch of mischief. The dark eyes and black hair might have come from a remote Spanish ancestor, but the generous, laughing mouth echoed his father. Max Danton had been a ne'er-do-well in his youth and wasn't much better now, according to the woman who loved him and had borne his children.

"And you're just as bad," she often reproved Luke. "It's time you got a proper job."

Owning two restaurants and having his own spot on cable television didn't count as a proper job in her book. Luke simply grinned at her criticisms. He loved his mother, while seldom heeding a word she said.

When he'd finished showering, he pulled on a pair of slacks and went back down to the kitchen. Dominique was already there, padding about, dressed in his best silk robe, and Luke moved to forestall her. He hated anyone else in his kitchen, just as an artist would dislike anyone tampering with his brushes.

"What time is it?" she yawned.

"Nearly midday! Hell, how did we sleep so late?"

"We didn't leave that nightclub until four," she

said, leaning against his chest, her eyes closed. "Then, when we got back—"

He grinned. "Yes," he said slowly, and they both laughed.

"Where do you keep the coffee?" she asked. "I can never remember."

"I'll make it," he said hastily, guiding her to a chair. "You sit down and let me wait on you."

She gave him a sleepy smile. "Not too much cream, please."

"As though I didn't know how to care for your figure by now," he said, starting to grind coffee.

She opened the robe wide, giving him a grand-stand view of her perfect shape. "It takes work to keep it like this," she observed.

He grinned. "Cover yourself up. I'm still worn-out after last night."

"No, you're not. You're never worn-out, Luke." She came up behind him and put her arms about him, pressing close in a way that nearly made him drop a spoon. "And I'm not worn-out, either—at least, not with you."

"I noticed that," he said, smiling, as some of the riper moments of the night came back to him.

"We go so well together—in every way." When he didn't answer she gave him a squeeze and per-sisted, "Don't you think so?"

Luke was glad she couldn't see his face right then. A life spent avoiding commitment had left him with antennae on permanent red alert. They were yelling now, warning him where this conversation was lead-ing, telling him that the next few moments would be crucial if his pleasant life was to remain pleasant.

"I know we go perfectly together in one way,"

he said lightly. Turning, he kissed the tip of her nose. "And who needs more?"

She pouted. "Sooner or later, everyone needs more."

Oh, Lord, she's going to take it right down to the line!

"Not this baby," he said, still keeping his tone friendly. He kissed her again, this time on the lips. "Let's not spoil a beautiful friendship."

She let it drop, but he didn't think it would be for long. He knew Dominique's awesome willpower. It had gotten her onto the books of the best modeling agency in Los Angeles. It had gotten her the plum jobs by methods that, Luke suspected, wouldn't bear scrutiny. What Dominique wanted, Dominique got. And now, it seemed, she wanted to tie him down.

His heart quailed at the thought of the coming battle. He wasn't afraid he would lose, because where his survival was concerned he had reserves of stubbornness that surprised people who'd seen only his laughter and cheerful kindness. But it seemed such a waste to be fighting when they could be doing other things.

Fight? Hell, no! He never fought with women. There were other ways to let them know where he stood. Subtle ways that left them still feeling friendly enough for a night of pleasure.

Luke both liked and adored women, not merely their bodies but the way their minds worked. He was enchanted by their oddities, their strange little secrets, and the way one of them would unconsciously teach him lessons that he could apply to others.

There wasn't one of his lovers who wouldn't welcome him back to her bed with glee. He wasn't conceited about this; he was profoundly, humbly grateful for their generosity. He wanted to go on being grateful. And no man was grateful for a ball and chain.

Subtlety. That was it!

"You poor darling," he said, kissing her tenderly. "Take this coffee and go back to bed while I make you something very special to eat."

"What do you mean, 'poor darling'? I don't need to go back to bed."

"Don't you? You look a little sleepy still."

"You mean I look tired?" she squealed in horror.

"No, no, just sleepy," he soothed. "And it's no wonder, after last night. You were just great."

"Well, I know what you like," she cooed, moving her hands over his skin.

"Don't do that," he begged, giving a skillful performance of a man afraid of being physically roused. Actually the reverse was true. Now that he knew what was on her mind, his senses seemed to have shut down, as they always did when he heard wedding bells. But it wouldn't be kind to let her suspect this. And Luke always tried to be kind.

Gently but firmly he led her back up the stairs, murmuring, "Go and snuggle up, baby, and let me pamper you."

He knew that was the offer no woman could refuse. And it would buy him a little time.

Maybe an hour. If he was lucky.

After he'd coaxed Dominique under the covers he returned to the balcony, looking up into the sky, silently imploring the angel who protected funloving bachelors to fly low over his nest.

From far off he could hear the faint sound of a

plane preparing to land at LAX. But somehow, he doubted if his good angel was aboard.

Ladies and gentlemen, British Airways flight 279 from London to Los Angeles will be landing in twenty minutes. It is 12:10 p.m. local time, and the temperature is seventy-five degrees....

Ten-year-old Josie looked back from where she was glued to the window. "Mummy, we took off at half past nine in the morning, and we flew for eleven hours. How can we land at half past twelve?"

Pippa yawned and stretched as far as conditions allowed. "Los Angeles is eight hours behind London, darling. I explained it all with the map."

"Yes, but it's different when it's real."

"That's true." Inwardly Pippa was working out how long it would be until she could have a good cup of tea.

Josie was doing calculations. At last she sorted it out to her own satisfaction. "We've been flying backward," she said triumphantly.

"I suppose we have."

"You see, you *can* time travel."

Flying backward, not eight hours but eleven years. Flying backward to revisit the naive girl of eighteen whose heart ruled her head, who'd loved one man totally, knowing that he only loved her casually.

Turn time back to the moment before she'd met Luke Danton. There she was, standing in the basement corridor of the Ritz Hotel, lost, wondering which way to go, trying the first door she saw, finding herself in the kitchen, where she had no right to be. And there was the handsome, laughing young man grabbing her arm, scooting her out, practically ordering her to meet him later.

Hurry past that door, quickly, while you still can. Run to the end of the passage and there's a flight of stairs. Now you'll never know he exists. Turn time back and be safe.

Safe. No Luke. No blazing, ecstatic four months. No anguished loneliness. No glorious memories. No darling, wonderful Josie.

She pushed open the door. And there he was....

It was crisis time.

Of course, he could always say bluntly, "No wedding! No way! And goodbye!" But Luke hated to hurt people, and he was fond of Dominique. He just didn't want to marry her.

He suspected a connection between this and a recent crisis in her life. After being a top model for six years, Dominique had been stunned to lose out on a job she really wanted.

To someone younger.

She was staggeringly beautiful, but she was an old lady of twenty-six, and the writing was on the wall.

She hadn't told Luke about the job, but he'd heard via the grapevine, and now he had a wry, good-natured awareness that his personal charm was not the only issue here. He didn't blame her. It was a tough world. Even the lovely face on your pillow could be working an angle, and Luke, who'd worked a few angles in his time, was relaxed about it.

But yielding to it was another matter.

His mind drifted to the one person, apart from his parents, who hadn't been trying to get something out of him: who had even refused his conscience-stricken offer of marriage, bless her heart!

Funny, kooky little Pippa, as crazy as he was himself, who'd made his months in London an enchanted time and seen him on his way with a smile and a wave.

He knew he'd been her first lover, and it still made him smile to remember how she'd enjoyed sex as though it were a box of chocolates. She'd jumped into bed with a whoop, unrestrained in her delight, warm and generous, as eager to give pleasure as to receive it. He hoped—yes, he really hoped—that she'd since found a man who could satisfy her as much as he had himself.

Who did he think he was kidding?

She'd even been cool about the discovery that she was pregnant. He was back home in Los Angeles by that time, but she'd dropped him a line. He'd telephoned her and dutifully suggested marriage, as he was an old-fashioned boy at heart. Pippa had thought that was very funny, he remembered. People didn't have to get married these days. Of course she wanted to keep the baby, but who needed Luke?

He hadn't been thrilled by her way of putting it, but it left him free and with a clear conscience. He'd thought of going over to see her, but flying was expensive, and it would be more sensible to send her the money. So he did that, and had done so ever since.

She still lived in his mind as the crazy kid with the wicked sense of humor that he'd known then. There were photographs to tell him what she looked like now, but they were somehow unreal beside the vividness of his memories.

He realized that he was smiling as that daft, quarrelsome, delightful female danced through his brain. She'd been so passionate about everything that she was exhausting to be with: passionate about her dreams, about food, about every tiny little argument. And she'd argued endlessly! He'd had to kiss her to shut her up. And then there had been no way to stop until he'd explored the whole of her glorious, vibrant body and discovered that she was passionate about him, as well.

Pippa knew she'd done everything the wrong way. It had been crazy to decide to go to Los Angeles one minute and book for the first available seats the next.

Now here she was, weary from the long flight, with an inner clock that said it was nearly midnight, the hardest part still to come and the day barely started. And since she hadn't warned Luke she was coming, he might not even be there.

Oh, why didn't she think before she did these impulsive things?

It was Jake's fault. And Harry's and Paul's and Derek's. They should have stopped her, especially Jake, who was supposed to be the sensible one. Instead he'd come up with the name of a friend in the airline who could get her a couple of heavily discounted tickets.

Paul and Derek had checked her medicines repeatedly and given her a list of rules for taking care of herself. Harry had driven her and Josie to the airport in his old car. And they'd all come along because they couldn't let her go so far away without waving her off.

If only her bags would appear on the carousel soon. She seemed to have been standing here for ages. She took a deep breath to disguise the fact that she was growing breathless, hoping Josie wouldn't notice. But Josie was bouncing about in excitement, eager to be the first to spot their luggage.

"There it is, Mummy! Over there."

"Don't rush." Pippa restrained her daughter from dashing over and trying to haul the bags off. "Wait for them to reach us."

Josie shook her head so that her long, red-brown hair swung jauntily. "I hate waiting. I like things to happen now."

"Then there'd be nothing left for later, and then what would you do?" Pippa teased her fondly.

"I'd make something happen later. I can make anything I like happen."

It always gave Pippa a pang when her daughter talked like that, for she remembered someone else who'd thought life was his to invent as he pleased. And he had been right.

Looking around made her realize how far she'd traveled, in more than miles, since she'd left England. This wasn't just a part of another country, but another world, another dimension.

Everyone looked so good. Where was the leavening of dowdiness that existed in any other population? Where were the overweight, the plain? They couldn't all be wanna-be movie stars, surely?

What had Luke said once?

"The cream of the crop came out West to get into the movies, and when they didn't, they stuck around and married each other. What you see on the streets is the third generation."

So much beauty was unnerving, like finding your-self in one of those episodes of *Star Trek* where nobody could crew a spaceship if they didn't look good enough to wear short skirts or skintight suits.

She'd dressed sensibly for the long flight, in old jeans and a sweater. Now being sensible felt like a crime.

At twenty-nine Pippa was tall and slim, with red-dish brown, shoulder-length hair that curved natu-rally and a heart-shaped face. She had large, lumi-nous eyes and a wide mouth that had always laughed easily. Her charm lay in that laughter and in the hint in her eyes that it came from way down deep inside her.

But she hadn't laughed so much recently, not since the doctor had said, "Pippa, I have to be hon-est with you..." And just now she felt as though she might never laugh again.

At last she had their baggage, they were safely through Immigration and could head for the airport hotel.

"Why couldn't we just stay with Daddy?" Josie wanted to know as they unpacked.

"Because he doesn't know we're coming, so he won't be ready for us."

It didn't take long to put everything away, and then Josie wanted to be up and going. They found a cab, and Pippa gave the driver Luke's address. "Will it take long?"

"'Bout ten minutes," he told her.

Only ten minutes, and she hadn't yet decided what she was going to say to Luke when he opened the door and saw her standing there with his daugh-ter. Why hadn't she warned him they were coming?

Because he might have vanished, said a wry voice in her mind. The Luke she'd known eleven years ago had been delightful, but the words *serious* and *responsible* weren't in his vocabulary. *Kind* was there. So were *charming* and *generous.* So, for that matter, were *fun, magical,* and *warm-hearted.* But *commitment* might never have been invented, for all he'd heard of it.

Which was why, although he'd paid generously toward his daughter's support, he had never seen her. And that was why they had crossed the Atlantic now, for Pippa was determined that he should meet his child before—she checked the thought there. She was good at not thinking beyond that point. Before Josie grew up too fast, she amended.

She had made the decision and put it into action without giving herself time to think—or to lose her nerve, as she admitted. Now here they were, almost at Luke's house. And the enormity of what she'd done was beginning to dawn on her.

If she could have turned around and gone right back home, she would have done so. But the cab was slowing down....

The heart of Luke's home was the kitchen, a stunning workplace that he'd designed himself, knocking a large hole in a wall so that it could run the whole length of the house.

There were five sinks, so that he was never far from running water, three burners, two ovens and a microwave. Every one of them was the latest, the most sophisticated technology, a mass of knobs that might have seemed excessive on the deck of a spaceship. People who knew Luke only superficially were always surprised by the precision of his kitchen. His looks were the tousled variety, as if he'd just gotten out of bed, and his personal entanglements might tactfully be described as untidy. But the kitchen, where he worked, was a miracle of organization.

In one corner he had a desk and a computer. He switched it on now and got online to Luke's Place, the restaurant he'd opened with such pride five years ago. The password got him into the accounts, where he could see that last night's takings were nicely up. A visit to Luke's Other Place, open only a year, produced an equally satisfying result.

His Web site showed a pleasing number of hits since yesterday, when his cable show, Luke's Way, had gone out. It was a cooking program, and since the first show, eighteen months ago, the ratings had soared. It was broadcast twice a week, and his site, always busy, was deluged in the hours afterward.

He briefly glanced at his e-mail, found nothing there to worry about and a good deal to please him. Then he noticed something that made him frown.

The e-mail he'd sent to Josie last night hadn't been collected on the other end. And that was unusual for Josie, who was normally a demon at reading his mail and coming back at him.

For a man who'd never met his daughter, Luke could say he knew her strangely well. He paid generously for her support. He had an account with the best toy store in London, and for Christmas and Josie's birthday, he would call and ask a pleasant sales assistant to select something suitable for her age and send it to her.

Twice a year he received a letter from Pippa,

thanking him for the gifts, giving him news of Josie and sometimes sending photographs. He could see how his daughter was growing up, looking incredibly like her mother. But she'd remained somehow unreal, until the day, a year ago, when he'd collected the e-mail that had come through his Web site and found one that said simply,

I'm Josie. I'm nine. Are you my pop? Mummy says you are. Josie.

The way she wrote *Mummy* in the English style, rather than *Mommy* in the American, told him this was real. When he'd recovered from the shock he e-mailed back, "Yes, I am." And waited. The answer came quickly.

Hallo, Pop. Thank you for the bike.

"You're welcome. How did you find me?"

Surfed until I found your Web site.

"On your own?"

Yes. Mummy's all thumbs.

Her initiative and bravado delighted him. It was exactly what he would have done at the same age, if Web sites had existed then. They began a correspondence of untroubled cheerfulness, save for one moment when he begged, "Please stop calling me Pop. It makes me sound like an outboard motor."

Sorry, Papa!

"'Dad' will do, you little wretch!"

At last Pippa had realized what was up, and entered the correspondence. Oddly, he found her harder to "talk" to. She still lived in his mind as a crazy, delightful girl. The woman she'd become was a stranger. But he persevered. She was the mother of his child, and he owed her. Their interchanges were cordial, but he was happier with Josie.

Recently he'd received a large photograph show-ing mother and daughter, sitting together, smiling at him. She was a great-looking kid, he reckoned.

Impulsively he pulled open the drawer where he kept the picture, took it out and grinned. Across the bottom was written, "Love to Daddy, Pippa and Jo-sie."

The last two words were in a different hand, large and childish.

That's my girl! he thought.

He began to replace the photograph, then some-thing stopped him. He drew it closer, studying the faces and the all-important words. An idea had come to him. It grew and flourished.

Wicked, he thought guiltily.

But his hands were already putting the picture in a prominent position. Not prominent enough. He changed it. Then he changed it back.

Wicked. Yes, definitely. But effective.

The good angel had come to his rescue again.

Inspired, he got to work on the perfect breakfast for a model. It was also a new recipe he'd invented for his restaurants. There was nothing like killing two birds with one stone, he told himself.

Onions, red wine vinegar, lettuce, fruit pieces, masses of strawberries, alfalfa sprouts. He laid them all out, then started on the salad dressing. This was going to be a work of art.

He could hear Dominique moving about upstairs, the sound of the shower. He prepared coffee and laid the breakfast bar to tempt a lady. He was a master of presentation.

Her eyes gleamed when she saw the trouble he'd

taken for her, and she gave him her most winning smile.

"Darling Luke, you're so sweet."

"Wait until you see what I've created for you," he said, pulling out a high stool and seeing her into it with a flourish. He laid the beautiful dish before her. "Less than two hundred calories, but full of nourishment."

"Mmm! Looks delicious." She put the first forkful into her mouth and made a face of ecstasy. "Heaven! And you invented it just for me."

And for the customers who would pay $25 a throw, and a few hundred thousand people who watched every Tuesday and Friday.

"Just what a hard-working model needs," he assured her. "Only three grams of fat. I measured each gram personally."

"What about each calorie?"

"All 197 of them."

She chuckled. "Oh, Luke, darling, you are a fool. It's why I adore you so madly. And you adore me, too, don't you? I can tell by the way you like to do things for me."

Sensing the conversation straying into dangerous waters again he filled her coffee cup and kissed the end of her nose.

But Dominique wasn't to be diverted. "As I was saying earlier, we go together so perfectly that it seems to me…" Just in time her eyes fell on the picture. Luke breathed a prayer of heartfelt relief.

"I've never seen that before," Dominique said, frowning.

"What—oh, that? I just had it out for a moment," Luke said quickly, moving as if to hurry the picture away, but actually relinquishing it into her imperiously outstretched hand.

"'Daddy'?" she echoed, reading the inscription. "You been keeping secrets, Luke? Is this your ex-wife?"

"No, Pippa and I weren't married. I knew her in London when I worked there eleven years ago. She still lives there."

"The child doesn't look anything like you. How do you know she's yours?"

"Because Pippa wouldn't have said she was if she wasn't. Besides, Josie and I talk over the Internet."

The supreme idiocy of this last remark burst on him only when it was too late. Dominique laid down the picture and regarded him very, very kindly.

"You talk on the Internet, and therefore she must carry your genes? I guess it beats DNA testing."

"I didn't mean that the way it came out," he said hastily.

"Darling, don't treat me like a fool."

No. Big mistake. Dominique's eyes were sharp as gimlets. They always were when she was in an acquisitive mood, he realized.

"Josie's mine," he repeated. "We have a very good relationship—"

"Over the Internet? Boy, you're really a close father, aren't you?"

"Considering we live on different continents, I'm a very close father," he said, stung.

"Luke, honestly, there's no need for this."

"What do you mean?"

"I mean that this child is no more your daughter than I am. You've probably never even met her mother. I expect you picked this up in some junk shop and wrote the inscription yourself. It was a clever idea putting 'and Josie' in different writing, but you were always a man who thought of the details.''

He took a long, nervous breath. This wasn't going right. He grasped her hand.

''Dominique—sweetheart—''

''Luke, it's all okay. I understand.''

''You...do?''

''It's natural for you to be a little scared at first. You've avoided commitment for so long, and now that things are changing, well—I guess it's all strange to you. But you show me in a thousand ways what I mean to you, and I can hear the things you don't say aloud.''

Luke gulped. When a woman got to hearing things a man hadn't said, he was in big trouble.

''Dominique...I swear to you that picture is genuine. Josie is my child, and Pippa is the very special lady who bore her—''

''Shh!'' She laid a beautifully manicured finger over his lips. ''You don't have to keep this up. We understand each other too well for pretenses.''

Luke couldn't speak. Now he knew how a drowning man felt when he was going down for the third time.

It was the perfect moment for a shadow to appear outside the back door, for a tap on the frosted glass, for him to open the door, for Pippa to be standing there with Josie, and for Josie to hurl herself at him with a cry of *''Daddy!''*

Chapter Two

The first words Luke Danton had ever spoken to Pippa eleven years before were, "Get out of here, quick!" after she'd barged into the kitchen of London's Ritz Hotel, where he'd been working.

He'd followed it up by grasping her elbow and hurrying her out of the door about as ungallantly as possible.

"Hey!" she objected.

"I didn't want you to be in trouble, and you would have been. You had no right to be in there."

"How do you know I haven't?"

"Because you're a chambermaid. I've seen you coming to work, and I asked about you."

"Oh," she said, taken aback.

"What time do you finish?"

"In an hour."

"Me, too. I'll meet you in the park, on the bench

near the entrance. Don't be late.'' He was gone before she could answer.

She scooted back to her own work, indignant, or trying to be. Suppose she didn't want to meet him in the park? He had an almighty cheek. But he also had laughing eyes and a vibrant presence, not to mention being tall and handsome. In fact, she didn't mind at all that he'd been asking about her.

After work she quickly changed out of her uniform and into her normal clothes. Not that most people would have called them "normal." They were young and crazy and turned heads wherever she went. The tight orange jeans shrieked at the purple cowboy boots. The big floppy hat was deep blue, and the multicolored sweater went with everything almost, and nothing exactly. She was eighteen and sassy. She could carry it off.

She checked herself in the mirror, pushing back a strand of her red-brown curly hair. Then she ran all the way to Green Park, the huge swath of grass and trees that stretched behind the hotel. It annoyed her to realize that she was actually hurrying so as not to miss him.

Glorious as a peacock, she sat on a bench that gave her a good view of the path he would have to take, and waited.

And waited.

And waited.

She leaned back, resting one elegantly booted ankle over the other knee, the picture of impish nonchalance. After a while she changed legs.

And waited.

At the end of an hour she was in a temper, less with him than with herself for still being there. Fum-

She added provocatively, "After all, most of you are descended from us."

"Not guilty," he said at once. "My ancestors are French, Spanish and Irish. If there are any British in that tree they're hidden in the closet with all the other skeletons. Now, come upstairs and eat."

His room consisted of a bed, a table, two chairs and shelves full of cookery books. In these shabby surroundings he gallantly pulled out a chair for her and served up the meal with as great a flourish as if they were in the Ritz dining room.

"What were you doing down there, anyway?" he wanted to know.

"I just wanted to look at the kitchens, to know what I'm aiming for."

"And what's that?"

"I'm not really a chambermaid," she confided. "I'm actually the world's greatest cook in disguise. Well, I will be, when I've finished learning. I'm going to be so great that one day the Ritz will beg me to return, to reign over its kitchen. And people will come from far and wide to taste my creations."

Luke was a good listener, and soon she'd told him everything, especially about her mother, her most precious memory.

"She was a fantastic cook. She'd have liked to be a chef, but she got married instead. Women did in those days," she said, speaking as though it was a distant age instead of twenty years ago. "And all my dad wanted was fish and chips, egg and chips, beans and chips."

"Chips? Oh, you mean French fries."

"I mean chips," she said firmly, trying to not respond to his grin. If she died for it she wouldn't let him tease a rise out of her. Well, not that easily, anyway.

"If she offered him anything imaginative he'd say, 'What's this muck?' and storm off to the pub. So she started teaching me how to cook properly. I think it was her only pleasure in life. We used to plan how I'd go to cookery college. She got an extra job so that she could save up to give me a start. But it was too much for her. We didn't know it then but she had something wrong with her heart. Mitral stenosis, the doctor said. It killed her."

For a moment her pixie face was sad, but she recovered.

"Rough deal," Luke said sympathetically. And through the conventional words she could sense the real kindness.

"Yes. The next thing I knew, Dad got married again, and suddenly I had a stepmother called Clarice, who loathed me."

"Real Cinderella stuff."

"Well, to be fair, I returned the compliment with interest. She used to call me Philippa," she added with loathing. "It wasn't enough that I never had time to do my homework because she developed a headache whenever there was any dusting to be done, but she actually addressed me as Philippa."

"A hanging offense," Luke said gravely.

"Yeah!"

"Any wicked stepsisters?"

"One stepbrother. Harry. But he made enough mess for ten and expected me to be his slave.

"When I mentioned going to college, Clarice glared at me and said, 'Where do you think the money for that's coming from? You've got grand ideas, think you're better than everyone else.'

"I argued, though you'd think I'd have known better by then. I said most people went to college these days. She sniffed and said, 'Not Harry.' And I said that since Harry was a moron *that* didn't come as a surprise, and *she* said I was an insolent little cow, and *I* said—well, you get the drift."

He was chuckling. "I wish I'd been there to see it. I'll bet you're a heckuva fighter."

"I am," she said, stating the simple truth.

"What about your mom's savings?"

"Dad took them. I remember him looking at the bank passbook and saying, 'I knew the bitch was hiding money from me!' I think he spent most of it on a honeymoon with Clarice."

"Wasn't there anyone to stick up for you?"

"Frank, my mother's younger brother, had a go at Dad. But Dad just told him to mind his own business. What could he do? I stuck it until I left school, then I got out."

"Cheered on by the dreadful Clarice?"

"No, she was furious. She'd got it all planned for me to work in her brother's grocery store for slave wages, and go on doing all the housework." Pippa's eyes gleamed with mischief. "I told her where she could put that," she said, with such wicked relish that Luke laughed out loud.

"I'll bet you did!" he said admiringly.

"She said she'd never heard such disgraceful language. I told her she'd hear it again if she didn't get out of my way. She screamed at me while I was packing, down the stairs, through the front door and all the way to the bus station.

"She said I'd come to a bad end in London, and I'd be crawling back in a week. I told her I'd starve first. I got on the bus and watched Clarice getting smaller and smaller until she vanished from my life and I vanished from hers. I've kicked the dust of Encaster off my feet, and it's staying off."

"Encaster? Don't think I've heard of it."

"Nobody's heard of it except the people who live there, and most of them wish they hadn't. It's about thirty miles north of London, very small and very dreary."

"Didn't your dad want you home?"

"I called him at his work once to let him know I was all right. He told me to 'stop being an idiot' and come back, because Clarice was giving him a hard time about it. That was all he cared about. If he'd been just a little bit concerned about me I'd have told him where I was. But he wasn't. So I didn't. That was the last time I talked to him. I'm still in touch with Frank, but he and Dad aren't speaking. He won't give me away."

"So you came to seek your fortune in London? At sixteen? Good for you, kid! Did you find the streets paved with gold?"

"They will be, one day. I do cookery courses in the evenings, and when I've got some diplomas I'll get a job as a cook. Then I'll do more courses, get a better job, and so on, until the gourmets of the world are beating a path to my door."

"S'cuse me, ma'am, but it's *my* door they're going to beat a path to."

"Well, I expect there'll be room for both of us," she conceded generously.

"You mean the three of us, don't you?" he asked

with a grin. "You, me and that colossal ego of yours. They'll have to build somewhere just to house it."

"And the rest! Everyone knows Americans can't cook."

"Can't— May you be forgiven! And since you come from the nation that eats French fries—"

"Chips!"

"—with everything, doesn't think food is properly cooked unless it's swimming in grease, and can't make decent coffee—"

"All right, all right, I give in." She threw up her hands in mock surrender, then pointed to her plate. "This is really delicious, I'll admit that."

"All my own invention. When I've got it perfect I'll present it to the head chef."

"Oh, great! Now I'm a guinea pig. If I don't drop dead after eating this you'll know it's safe to offer it to the Sultan of Thingy and the Duke of Whatsit?"

"Something like that," he admitted with a grin.

She saw him regarding her outfit and said, "Nice, huh?"

"Love it, and the purple thing you were wearing when I saw you the other day."

Pippa chuckled. "The head housekeeper nearly fainted. She couldn't get me out of it and into my uniform fast enough. But I don't like people to overlook me."

"No danger of that. How do you afford fashion and pay for classes, as well?"

"I make my own fashion from other people's rejects. The jeans came from a rummage sale, the boots had been reduced five times because the color frightened people, the hat came from an Oxfam shop, and I knit the sweater from remnants.''

He grinned, enchanted.

His own story delighted her. He was, as she'd guessed, American, from Los Angeles, and his life seemed to have revolved around sun, sea and sand. His passion was cookery and the only books he ever opened were recipes. Beyond that there wasn't a thought in his head apart from swimming, body-surfing, eating, drinking and generally having a good time. There had been so little fun in Pippa's life that this young man, who seemed to make almost a religion of merriment, seemed to usher her to a new and magical world, one in which the light was always golden, the sensations exquisite and youth would last forever.

He had ambition, of a kind.

''I don't just want to be *a* cook, there are plenty of them,'' he explained. ''I want to be *the* cook, so I had to find something that would make me stand out from the others. I scraped together all the money I could and came to Europe, to work in some of the great hotels. I did six months in the Danieli in Venice, six in the George V in Paris, and now I'm doing the London Ritz. When my work permit's up I'll go back to Los Angeles as Luke of the Ritz. Hey, have you swallowed something the wrong way?'' For Pippa was doubled up and apparently choking.

''You can't do that,'' she spluttered when she could speak. ''*Luke of the Ritz?* Nobody will be able to eat for laughing.''

''Oh!'' he said, deflated. ''You don't think they'll be impressed?''

''I think they'll chuck tomatoes at you.''

The awful truth of this hit him suddenly and he began to laugh, too. The more he laughed, the more she laughed, and it became funnier and funnier.

If this were a romantic comedy, she thought, they would laugh until they fell into each other's arms. She found herself tingling with anticipation.

But Luke pulled himself together and said in a choking sort of voice, "It's late. I ought to be getting you home."

"It's not that late," she protested.

"It is when I have a 6 a.m. start. Come on."

He borrowed a battered old car from one of the other residents, and drove the couple of miles to the hostel where she lived. As he pulled up, Pippa waited for his arm around her shoulders, pulling her close, his lips on hers...

"Here we are," he said, pulling open the passenger door.

Reluctantly Pippa got out of the car. He came with her to the front door.

"See you tomorrow," Luke said, giving her a brief peck on the cheek. In a moment his taillights were vanishing around the corner, and she was left standing there, muttering some very unladylike words.

Pippa was proud of being a modern young woman, unshackled by the prejudices and restraints of outmoded convention, free to enjoy worldly delights on equal terms with men. If she wanted to smoke, drink and pursue the pleasures of the flesh, she had every right to do so.

That was the theory. The practice was more difficult. The only cigarette she had ever tried had been in a pub with a party of friends. She'd promptly had a violent coughing fit, upset a bowl of peanuts all over the floor and been ordered out by an exasperated publican. She hadn't tried again. It had tasted disgusting, anyway. So much for smoking.

Alcohol was also a problem. She could twirl a glass bravely, but more than a little of the cheap plonk, which was all she could afford, upset her stomach. So much for drinking.

Which left sex. And that wasn't working out brilliantly, either.

She'd naively imagined that London would be filled with attractive, lusty males, all eager to meet a liberated young woman. But a depressingly large number of them were middle-aged and boring. Too many of the young ones were studious, married or gay. They talked too much. Or too little. Or about the wrong things. It was like being back in Encaster.

She wasn't short of offers. A tall, delicately built young woman with a daft sense of humor, laughing eyes and legs up to her ears was always going to turn heads. It should have been, as the song said, a matter of picking "the height, the weight, the size." But the height was too often awkward, and the weight was usually excessive. So she passed up the chance to check the size.

After two years in London Pippa was virginal, exasperated and uneasily aware that as an advertisement for riotous living she was a miserable failure. At this rate she might as well be a Victorian maiden. It was very disheartening.

She wondered if it was too late to become a nun.

But from the moment she met Luke everything changed. He won by default because he was none of the dreary things the others were. Also because his voice had a vibrant note she'd never heard before, and it produced a quickening of excitement in her. He won, too, because his eyes teased and tempted her, because his mouth was wide and mobile, and it could be tender, amused, or firm when his stubbornness was aroused.

But mostly he won because just being in the same room with him could induce a fever in her. Plus, the rotten so and so had never shown any sign of wanting to entice her into his bed. It was an insult that she couldn't let pass.

What made it more galling was that everyone at work simply assumed they were sleeping together. Luke had a reputation as a love-'em-and-leave-'em heartbreaker.

"He calls it traveling light," one of the other maids confided. "He was going out with Janice on the third floor. Everything was lovely until she invited him to a family wedding. Big mistake. He only called her once more and that was to tell her he had to do a lot of overtime, so they'd better cool it."

Ears flapping, Pippa listened to all the gossip and made mental notes of what not to do. Deciding what *to* do was harder.

He never actually asked her out, but their shifts were roughly the same, and whoever finished first would wait for the other. Then they would stroll home, his arm about her shoulders, while Luke talked like a crazy man and Pippa tried not to be too aware of how badly she wanted him to stop talking and start kissing.

She decided to be subtle about it. Instead of Luke always doing the cooking, she would prepare an intimate supper, at his place, candlelight, soft music, and one thing would lead to another.

It was a disaster.

It might have worked with any other man, but Luke was constitutionally unable to sit quiet while somebody else cooked for him. With the best will in the world he couldn't refrain from suggesting that she turn the gas down and give this dish or that just a *little* more time.

In the end she stormed out. It was that or throw the lot over him.

Next day he was waiting for her with a posy and a heartfelt apology.

"I did you an injustice, didn't I?" he said humbly. "You weren't really going to do the crème caramel like that."

The quarrel that resulted from this remark took three days to heal. But nobody could quarrel for long with a man as sweet tempered as Luke. When he realized she wasn't going to make the first move he waited for her to leave the hotel and approached her with a finger pressed over his mouth.

"Good evening," she said frostily.

He made no sound, but pointed to the silencing finger with his other hand.

"I'm going home now," she declared.

But it was impossible. Whichever direction she took he was there before her, blocking off her exit, herding her toward the boarding house like a sheepdog with an awkward lamb.

"I don't know what you think you're playing at," she said exasperated.

From his pocket he took a small notebook on

"Not in London," she said idiotically. She knew she was crazy, but she couldn't stop herself.

"It's just that there's something about you—something very sweet and young—that made me think—oh, hell!" Now it was his turn to be embarrassed, and Pippa seized her chance to regain the initiative.

"You know your trouble, Luke? You think too much. What a lot of fuss you make over something that's no big deal. The world is *full* of ships that pass in the night, and if...if people like each other..."

In later years, reliving that conversation, she'd heard the childish bravado and known that Luke must have heard it, too. He hadn't been fooled—of course not. But whatever defenses he'd rallied against her had collapsed in a heap. Suddenly she was in his arms, his fingers were working urgently on her buttons, and everything was happening as she had dreamed.

When he released her breasts she was almost ashamed of them. They were so proudly peaked, the nipples already firm, the aureoles dark, telling their own tale of the desire she'd been trying to hold back. What had happened to maidenly modesty? Then he laid his lips gently against one, teasing it with his tongue, and she thought, when she could manage to think at all, to hell with maidenly modesty!

As his tongue nudged the nipple softly back and forth she thought she might go out of her mind. How could anything feel like this, and how had she spent so long not knowing? So much time wasted! It was a conspiracy.

She took a long, trembling breath and dug her fingers into him as his lips and tongue continued their tormenting work. With every rasp the world shivered into glittering fragments, blinded her, faded, began again.

He undressed her slowly, removing garments as though there was plenty of time. Only his quickened breathing and the way his fingers shook as he eased off her jeans hinted at how frantically he was controlling himself until the right moment. Then her panty hose slid away, and at last she was naked.

He removed his own clothes in a hurry and chucked them on the floor without taking his eyes from Pippa.

"Hello," he said, smiling.

"Hello." She sounded breathless.

She'd never shown her body off to a man before, but she knew she could be proud of its slim, youthful lines, tiny waist and long flanks. Her breasts were small, firm and cheekily uptilted. She longed to ask him if he thought she was beautiful, but perhaps he was already letting her know in the loving way he stroked her smooth skin and traced the outline of her curves, murmuring appreciatively as he did so and sometimes stopping to bestow a light kiss before moving on.

She was almost shocked by the fierceness of her own sensations, as if her body was possessed by another being, one that had never heard of restraint. For a wild moment all the old precepts of childhood—don't grab—be patient—learn to wait—flashed through her head, and she knew they belonged to another world, not the world of thrilling, sensational delight Luke was offering her now. She was alive for the first time in her existence.

She reached for him, and it felt so good to be able to touch him all over at last. She'd tried so often to picture him without clothes, but nothing could match the reality of his lean, smooth body. She was at fever pitch. She wanted him so badly.

"Luke," she whispered, "you do want me, don't you?"

His answer came without words. Grinning, he drew back so that she could see the truth for herself, and there he was, proud and hard with the splendid, arrogant power of youth. And he was all hers.

"Luke," she cried in an agony of impatience.

"Yes, darling."

At last he parted her legs and settled between them. Then he was sliding easily into her, and it was beautiful, and she wanted him more and more. She wanted it never to stop. She wanted the whole world, and he was giving it to her. He thrust deeply and slowly, sending pleasure through every part of her body, starting with her loins and radiating out to her fingertips.

Then it happened. Something in the universe went *click* and everything fell into place. Instinct took over, guiding her perfectly. It was as though Luke had tossed her a dream and she'd caught it and run with it. Nobody had told her how, but her hips moved of their own accord, driving against him. The feeling of being able to heighten her own pleasure and his was thrilling, and when Luke responded by thrusting back more fiercely, she went into orbit.

As she felt the same happen to him, she threw back her head, almost caroling with joy. It was all true. Everything was true. There was magic in the world after all, and happiness and fulfillment and laughter and song. It was true. She was alive and glad and young, and it was all wonderfully, gloriously true.

He held her close as they came down from the heights. Pippa lay against him, blissfully happy, understanding now that all her rationalizing had been hot air. She could never have done this with Jack or Andy or Clive or any of the others. Because they weren't Luke.

He kissed the top of her head, but she could sense that he was troubled about something. "What is it?" she demanded. "Am I no good?"

"You're wonderful. It's just that I promised myself I wouldn't do this. And I guess I'm not very honest, because if I'd meant it I'd have stopped seeing you and put myself out of the way of temptation. I wanted you so much, and sooner or later I was bound to give in."

"But why shouldn't you?"

"Because of the way you are, because of the way I am. I won't stick around, Pippa. I never do. When my permit expires, I'm back off to Los Angeles, on my own. It's like you said—ships that pass in the night."

She shrugged. "I knew that. So what?" It was easy to say when the glorious months stretched out ahead.

"Well—you're special. You deserve a man who'll be there—"

"You mean Mr. Solid and Reliable, who'll march me to the altar and give me a semidetached house in the suburbs and a dozen kids? No, thank you! I left Encaster to escape him."

"If there's one thing I'm not, it's Mr. Solid and Reliable."

"If you were, we wouldn't be lying here like this."

How much of that brave talk had she meant, or thought she meant? And how much was just saying what she knew he wanted to hear? She never really knew. If he wanted her to be cool about it, then cool she would be. There were months to make him change his mind.

With her acute sensitivity to Luke's moods, Pippa began to see life through his eyes. On a walk in the park one evening, she couldn't help noticing the little family of two prematurely middle-aged parents and one demanding child.

"Daddy, listen to me—"

"In a minute, darling."

"No, now Daddy, now!"

The woman sounded testy. "It wouldn't hurt you to take some notice of your own daughter once in a while."

"I might if she'd shut up occasionally."

Luke grinned. "Poor sod!" he said. "Once he was a free man. Now he can't remember what it felt like."

Wearily the man looked down at the little tyrant. "All right, pet, what is it?"

"Come and look here. There's a caterpillar, a great big one."

Luke and Pippa strolled on, arms about each other, and the piercing voice seemed to follow them.

"Come and look *now*, Daddy. Daddy, Daddy, *Daddy!*"

Chapter Three

"Daddy, *Daddy, DADDY!*" Josie's voice rose a note higher on each word.

Give him his due, Pippa thought, Luke reacted magnificently, sweeping his daughter up into his arms and crying, "There's my special girl!" in a glad voice.

They surveyed each other, considering, sizing up. Pippa almost laughed at the uncanny mirror image of their attitudes. Their faces weren't alike but their movements, their way of holding their heads back at a slight angle that said "Oh, yeah?" were identical.

Luke deposited the child gently on the floor and turned to Pippa, arms open. As he pulled her close he muttered into her ear, "Bless you as an answer to a prayer."

Over his shoulder she saw Dominique, and things

began to fall into place. Not everything, but enough
to understand that Luke was "on the run" again.

He released her. "Pippa, my love, this is Dominique—a friend. Dominique, this is Pippa, who I
was just now telling you about."

All Pippa's antennae were on full alert and she
saw everything, even the very small tightening of
the other woman's mouth at "a friend."

Dominique stood with her robe slipping open just
enough to show that she was naked underneath. She
held out a beautifully manicured hand, surveying
Pippa in a way that was obviously meant to be in-
timidating. She smiled back, refusing to be awed.

"Better put some clothes on," Luke said, an arm
around Dominique's shoulders, urging her to the
door. "And don't you have an appointment in an
hour?"

"Three hours, actually," the model said glacially.

"Well, you don't want to be late, do you?" Luke
switched his attention to Pippa and Josie. "Where
are your bags?"

"At the airport hotel."

"You're not staying in any hotel," he said, outraged. "My family stays with me. I'll have the spare
room ready in no time. You'll love it."

"Thank you. As long as I'm not putting you
out—" this was to Dominique.

"Not at all," the other woman drawled, adding
with meaning, "*I* wasn't sleeping in the spare
room."

"I'm sure you weren't," Pippa said, meeting her
eyes evenly.

Luke had slipped away to talk to Bertha, who
cleaned for him and had just arrived. Dominique

lowered her voice, indicating the photograph. "Don't kid yourself, honey! That picture never appeared before today."

Pippa's lips twitched. "Really? He must have needed it very urgently—today."

"Oh, you're very funny! But I know a con when I see one."

"I'm sure you do. It takes one to know one, doesn't it?"

Dominique flounced away, too wise to answer this.

It might have been a lot worse, Pippa realized. As it was, she'd had a welcome better than her brightest hopes, even if it was because she was saving his skin. That reference to "my family" had been for Dominique's benefit of course, but it had been just what Josie needed to hear.

Luke returned, smiling, and placed his hands on her shoulders. "Let me look at you. Oh, Pippa, you're a sight for sore eyes."

"So I gathered," she teased.

"No, not just because of that. After all this time you're just—just my Pippa."

"Hey, what am *I?*" Josie demanded indignantly.

"You're my best girl," he said at once, and hugged her. "Now, first things first. Coffee, then the hotel."

"I'm hungry," Josie declared.

"Josie!" Pippa exclaimed. "Manners!"

"Of course she's hungry," Luke said. "Milk and strawberry salad."

"You can't put strawberries in a salad," Josie protested.

"You can, *chez* Luke."

Josie looked puzzled, and he explained, "*Chez* means *at the home of.* It's French. I use it when I want to impress people."

"You said milk," Josie reminded him in the accents of a starving orphan.

"Coming up!"

While he was finding the milk and pouring it for her, Bertha returned to say the room was ready. Pippa slipped away with her, while Luke got to work on the strawberry salad, collecting strawberries, raspberry vinegar, mint and lettuce.

"This is a concoction of Luke of the Ritz," he declared, lining up a selection of other fruits like a general inspecting his troop. "Sour cream," he added briskly. "That cupboard over there."

Josie moved fast and brought the cream, just right.

"Now some honey. That one."

She repeated the action, practically standing to attention when she'd delivered the honey.

"Who was Luke of the Ritz?" she asked. "You?"

"No, but I nearly was. Can you open that door next to the sink, please?" She did so, and he took out his electric blender.

"Why nearly?"

"Because your mommy thought people would die laughing. She was right, too." As he spoke he was washing the strawberries, then preparing to stem and halve them.

"I can do that," Josie said, taking a knife.

"Hey, no! That's too sharp for you." But he fell silent as he saw how efficiently she got to work. "Done it before, huh?"

"I help in the kitchen at home. Mummy says

don't touch sharp knives, but I can handle them, so I do, anyway.''

"Guess you do,'' he murmured, watching the neat little fingers flying and recalling another child who'd done what he wanted rather than what his mother said. ''And what does she say about that?''

"Well—'' Josie stopped for a moment to consider ''—she starts to say things like, 'Do as I tell you,' and 'Josie, did you hear me?' But then Jake puts his head around the door and says, 'Hey, Pip, I'm on early shift. Is it ready yet?' Or Harry gets upset because he's lost something important. Harry's always losing things that he says are important. Or Paul comes in covered in axle grease—Paul restores old cars—or Derek—''

"Whoa, hold on there! Who are all these guys?''

"They're our boarders, only they're friends, as well. They're all terribly fond of Mummy. I've done all the strawberries. What's next?''

"Lettuce. Give it a good wash.''

While she washed he got out some china plates, then she arranged lettuce leaves while he puréed some of the strawberries.

"Now for the honey, mint and sour cream,'' he declared dramatically, just as he did on his show.

But it wasn't the camera fixing its gaze on him, or the audience crowding the benches, laughing at his well-rehearsed but so spontaneous-seeming flourishes. It was a cheeky little girl with laughing eyes, regarding him with her head on one side, exactly as another girl had done once before. It gave him a strange turn.

In fact, everything about today was strange. Only a few hours ago he'd awoken next to a beautiful

model, the ultimate bachelor's dream. Suddenly he
was a father. Okay, Okay, he'd been a father for
years, but until this moment he hadn't *felt* like a
father. Now he did. And it felt good. Every man
should have a daughter, he reckoned, especially one
with long, curly red hair, a cheeky grin and her
mother's air of challenging everyone.

Once again Luke Danton had gotten lucky. The
world's goodies had fallen into his lap, just the way
they always did. And again, as always, he was grateful.

Luke's bathroom was modern luxury made to
look like Victorian basic: white tiles on the walls,
dark-red and brown decorative tiles on the floor, and
glowing brass fixtures. The effect was sumptuous.

After splashing water on her face Pippa sat down
while she dried herself, and took long breaths. She'd
cleared the first hurdle. It had been tough, but she'd
coped. She'd gotten over Luke long ago, but it was
never going to be easy seeing him again, being
physically close to him. Luke wasn't just a handsome face, or charm personified, although he was
both those things. He was a body that she still remembered during her lonely nights and a vibrant
presence and warm, laughing eyes.

He might have been dismayed to see her, and
she'd braced herself for that. But nothing had prepared her for the welcome she'd received, even if
she did know that Luke was being practical. Being
hugged close to him was unnerving, but she would
get over that. She had come here for Josie's sake,
and that was all that mattered.

She took a few more deep breaths, and when she

felt better she returned to the kitchen where Luke was dishing up. She was suitably impressed by the creation.

"One hundred and twenty calories, and four grams of fat," he explained. "I add that bit automatically now. People always seem to want to know."

"And it's delicious," Josie said blissfully. "Mummy, why don't we have strawberry salad?"

"Oh, sure," Pippa said wryly, "I can see Jake and Harry eating strawberry salad. If it doesn't have chips and fried bacon they doesn't want to know." She assumed an attitude. "'Hey, Pip, I've got a fourteen-hour shift. A man needs something to keep him going, know what I mean?'"

"Fourteen hours?" Luke echoed.

"Jake's just qualified as a doctor," Pippa explained. "Which means he lectures the rest of us about healthy eating and stuffs himself with stodge."

It was Josie who finished first, devouring Luke's helping as well as her own, then hopped up and down impatiently until they were ready to go to the hotel for the bags. For the short journey she sat in the back of Luke's Porsche, eyes popping at everything she saw. Luke and Pippa were together in the front.

"I still can't get my head around this," he said.

"You mean I shouldn't have come?" she asked quickly.

"No, I love surprises. And you were an answer to a prayer."

"Yes, I could see. What would you have done without me?"

"Lord knows," he said with a shudder. "But I didn't mean that. I meant you. You always did things without warning, like a firecracker. It's great to know you haven't changed."

"Well, perhaps I should have changed by now. I'm eleven years older, but I don't seem to be much wiser. You might have been living with that woman."

He gave a reminiscent grin.

"No way. Know something? The only woman I ever lived with was you."

She'd moved into the guest house with Luke. "Ma" Dawson, upon whom his charm had a powerful effect, had found them a room just big enough for two, just down the corridor from the kitchen. She was a kindly soul but a dreadful cook, something that she blamed vaguely on "me rheumatics," without ever explaining the connection. Pippa took over the cooking for three evenings, in addition to the two Luke had already been doing, and Ma gave them a heavy discount on the rent.

Pippa loved the happy-go-lucky atmosphere of the house. It stood a couple of blocks away from a big teaching hospital, and most of the residents were medical students. They lived on the edge of poverty, kept incredible hours without collapsing, studied a lot, ate and drank a lot and laughed a lot.

There were magic nights sitting up until the early hours discussing "Life" with a capital *L* with Angus and Michael and Liz and Sarah and George and anyone else who dropped in. She added her mite to the talk, snuggled in the curve of Luke's arm, relishing the warmth of his lean body, half hearing half sensing the beat of his heart.

He would sit there contentedly with her, but he said little. He was too busy living life to talk about it, and he hated analyzing abstractions. In fact, he hated abstractions.

Life reached Luke through his senses, through the taste of food, the smell of ingredients, what he felt against his skin and in his loins. To him the world was physical, tangible, and where it wasn't, he shrugged.

When he was bored with these talks he would nibble softly on her ear. Then they would slip away together, and the rest of the night would be even more magic.

She seemed to be floating through life in a blissful haze of newly discovered pleasure, so that everything that happened was sensual and lovely. This was true even of things that weren't directly connected with Luke, but a hundred times more true about things that were. She couldn't be in the same room with him without growing excited and impatient. When he was cooking she watched his hands. They were artist's hands, powerful and muscular, yet sensitive, too, and the mere sight of them could thrill her body, which carried the memories of their intimate touch.

At work she wore the sedate, respectable uniform of a chambermaid, but it told a lie. Beneath it she wasn't respectable at all. It made her laugh sometimes to think how shocked people would be if they knew her head was filled with thoughts of Luke, who wanted her as uncontrollably as she wanted him—Luke, in bed with her, naked and aroused. In thought she dwelt on every inch of him: how long and slim his flanks were; how firm his behind; how unexpectedly strong his hands; how big and hard he was inside her; how badly she wanted him there.

Once, at home, the urgency grew more than she could stand, and as soon as he closed the oven door, she fastened her lips on his in the fiercest kiss she'd ever given him—avid, devouring, voracious, gloriously shameless, both giving and demanding. With one hand she cupped his head, while with the other, began undressing him. After the first shock he'd responded avidly, drawing her swiftly out of the kitchen and along the corridor to their room. They barely had time to shut the door before they were pulling off each other's clothes, almost competing to see who could strip whom the fastest. She could never remember who'd won, but they were both naked before they hit the bed.

She pulled him over her with strong, determined movements. She wasn't fooling. She wanted Luke on the most basic, primitive level and no nonsense about it. Romance and candlelight were lovely in their place, but right now she would go crazy if she couldn't feel him inside her, completing her, filling her to satiation point.

At last she had her way. He was there, thrusting vigorously in the way she loved. She drove back against him, drawing him deep into her, knowing this excited him to madness. She loved his strength, the fierce power in his loins, his tirelessness. To match it she offered her craving for him that could never be satisfied for long, her delight in pleasing him as much as he pleased her.

Later she tormented herself with questions. Had

she spoiled things by being too forward, too eager, too always ready? Should she have held off, teased him, made him wonder about her? That might have been subtle and clever, but it would also have been a kind of deception that her passionately honest nature couldn't have managed. She was young and bursting with health. To enjoy sex with your lover seemed natural, like discovering the secret of life itself, or being given a Christmas present every day. And each day the present was a little different, a little better. But had her own gifts to him grown better? Or had he gradually become bored with her? She would always wonder. Or perhaps wondering was just a word for knowing the truth but not admitting it.

But there were other memories to set beside these, glorious nights when she'd lain naked in his arms while he worshipped her body by moonlight. And other nights when he acted like a clown, spicing passion with wit, making her laugh even while her body was in a fever. Once he'd said, "I'm trying to work out which part of you I like best. It's a tough decision because you have the most perfect breasts of any woman in the world."

As he spoke he was tracing a finger over the swell of her right breast, lingering over the nipple, teasing it until the excitement stormed along her nerves and it was all she could do to say, "You'd know, would you? About all the others?"

"Mmm—" he seemed to consider this "—maybe not *all* the others."

"But a good few?" she asked, torn between joking and jealousy.

"Enough to know that you're the best. Now hush, I'm concentrating."

She laughed and fell silent, enjoying herself as he treated the other breast to similar caresses until both nipples were proudly peaked. By now they were familiar with each other's bodies, and knew the touches that best pleased. He knew how she loved to be kissed all over, very, very slowly, deferring the ultimate moment of pleasure so that it would be all the more exquisite. She was excited by the thrill it gave him when she ran her fingers lightly over his chest, and down to where he was leaping up to her.

Although she enjoyed his admiration it soon brought her to such a pitch of excitement that she grew impatient and tried to incite him with her own caresses. But he suddenly went into clowning mode, and prevented her firmly and with dignity.

"Madam, please stop that," he said solemnly. "I've been reading a book about foreplay, and I want to practice."

"Was it useful—this book?" she asked, falling in with his game.

"Extremely," he informed her, poker-faced. "Now observe this next bit carefully, because afterward I'm going to ask you questions. And, hush! How can I create a romantic mood if you're giggling?"

He was lazily drifting his fingers along the insides of her thighs, reaching the top, lingering for a shattering moment, before drifting away again. She gasped and dug her fingers into his shoulders as her arousal grew more intense.

"Did the book explain—the significance of that gesture?" she murmured in his ear.

"It's supposed to put you in the mood."

"But if I told you I was already in the mood?"

He became prim. "Then I would say you were a very forward young woman, and I'd be shocked. And the book didn't warn me that you'd do *that*."

"I'm sorry!"

"I forgive you, but I've lost the place now. I'll check the index."

"You let go of me and you're dead."

"You're not being helpful at all," he complained. "I'm trying to learn the nuances. A man is supposed to be subtle, not just go at it like a bull at a gate. The manual promised that this would make you appreciate me more."

"I could hardly appreciate you more than I already do," she said, fingering the part of him she appreciated most at that moment and trying to guide it toward her. "Luke," she pleaded, "couldn't you skip the subtleties and just charge the gate?"

"Woman, where is your heart of romance?"

"Let's be romantic another time. Tonight I'm feeling very, very basic."

"In that case," he said, settling swiftly between her thighs, "let's charge the gate together."

And they did, taking it fast and furious, so that they ended up breathless and full of glory.

"I think," Pippa said between gasps, "that we demolished the gate that time."

Which made them both laugh so hard that they lost their sense of decorum for the second time that night and clasped each other in a state of fierce delight in which subtlety played no part. Even so, there was still tenderness. Luke entered her in the way she loved the most, slowly but strongly, prolonging the moment to the full so that she felt the hardness of him filling her up, completing her. And when she met his eyes she found a smile there. Not the laughter of before, when he'd been clowning, but a glow that told her they were at one. She smiled back, full of a joy that went beyond physical pleasure, and knowing that there was only him in all the world.

Pippa always remembered that night, because at some point sex became lovemaking. At least, that's what happened for her. How or when it changed, or why it happened just then, was a mystery. But what had been a joyous game with a prize every time, became deeper, more poignant. The prize was still there, as sweet as ever, but suddenly there was a price to be paid. This wasn't just the man who brought her sexual delight. He was the man who laid his head against her breast and fell asleep, as though he trusted her totally, so that she melted with tenderness and a mysterious pleasurable ache.

They had never spoken of love. It was all part of being in a modern relationship, with no strings. You each lived your own life and passed on. But suddenly love was there, awkward, inconvenient, getting in the way of your plans, and unwanted, since he was a man who wouldn't be tied down, and love equaled strings. Right?

But he was asleep now, so she could whisper, "Sorry, darling. I went back on the deal. I wish I could tell you, but you'd be scared stiff. Never mind. My problem, not yours. It's all a laugh, isn't it? Oh Luke, *Luke!*"

Among other things Pippa adored Luke for his sweet temper. The only time she could recall seeing

him disgruntled was when she was dressing to go
out one Saturday, without inviting him, or even telling him where she was going.

"The first Saturday we've both had off for ages
and you vanish," he grumbled. "*And* you're dressing up, as if it's somewhere special." He looked
suspiciously at the clinging jersey dress in a brilliant
cerise, that only she could have carried off. "It's not
like you to keep secrets."

"It's only a little secret."

"So what's the big deal about telling me?" He
scowled suddenly. "Who is he?"

"His name's Frank, and he's my uncle, and I'm
going to his wedding."

"Great!" he sulked. "I'm not good enough to
meet your family!"

"Don't be silly, darling. I just thought it would
bore you. A wedding, solid family gathering, men
in formal suits, women in hats. I know that sort of
thing gives you nightmares."

"I'd rather put up with it than not see you all
day."

"Luke, are you sure? You know what'll happen
if we go together—"

"People will simper and ask when you're going
to make an honest man of me. Don't worry, we'll
tell them you're keeping me as a pet. Will your father and Clarice be there?"

"No, they moved away a few months ago."

"So, let's be on our way." He kissed her. "If
you think I'm letting you go anywhere, looking so
pretty, without me, you're crazy."

From somewhere he produced a suit, borrowed

his friend's old car and they were soon on their way. Her heart was singing with joy. She hadn't invited him, determined not to repeat the mistake that had frightened him off other girlfriends. But he was coming, anyway, because he was jealous. He was actually jealous! It was too good to be true.

They reached Frank's house just before noon and found him calm and well prepared. He owned a small corner shop that was modestly prosperous. Gravity had settled on him early in life, and he looked ten years older than his actual age, which was thirty.

Pippa gave him an exuberant hug, and he kissed her with quiet affection. When the introductions were over she demanded, "Why aren't you pacing the floor with nerves, like a normal bridegroom?"

"What is there to be nervous about?" he asked, mildly surprised. "Elly's organized everything down to the last detail. She's wonderful at that."

"Is that the best he can say about the woman he's marrying?" Luke muttered in her ear.

"Frank doesn't wear his heart on his sleeve," she muttered back. But aloud she couldn't resist saying, "Honestly, Frank, it's not decent to be so cool and composed. You might at least be gnawing your fingers about whether Elly will show up at the church, or fretting that you aren't good enough for her."

He looked bewildered for a moment, then smiled and gave her shoulders a squeeze. "You will have your little joke," he said tolerantly. "I'm so glad you're here, my dear."

Elly was a plump, comfortable widow, a couple of years his senior. Pippa had met her before and liked her, thinking how perfectly she suited him.

part her thighs. Then he was there between them, finding her, sliding into her. She was almost sobbing with pleasure, wrapping her legs and arms about him with fierce intent. Of all the delights in the world there was only this that really mattered, having your man inside you, feeling the heat of him, smelling his warm, spicy skin, giving yourself to him a thousandfold and taking from him all he had to give. When her moment of release came, she made a sound like a cry of triumph.

As they lay blissfully together afterward, Pippa suddenly exploded with uncontrollable laughter.

"What? What?" he asked, already beginning to laugh with her.

"What we just did—" she choked.

"You've never found it funny before."

"No, not us—Frank and Elly—"

He buried his face against her, and making muffled sounds while his shoulders shook. "Don't," he begged at last. "I can't laugh any more. It hurts. Anyway, perhaps they won't bother."

"Oh, they will. They want lots of children, and Frank believes that everything should be done properly. I suppose we shouldn't laugh. It isn't kind."

"We're not doing them any harm," he gasped. "And he's such a—oh, Lord, perhaps I should have loaned him my book."

"Then he could make a list—and—and tick it—as he—"

And they were off again, clinging to each other in an agony of mirth. The world was theirs, and from their lofty perch of bliss they could afford a little pity for middle-aged people who thought they knew what life was about.

Chapter Four

At the start, four months had seemed to stretch out endlessly ahead, time enough for Luke to see that they belonged together forever. But then four months became three, two, then one, and suddenly it was only a couple of weeks before his work permit expired.

He sat up in bed beside her one night, breathless from the fray, and said, "Oh, baby, I'm going to miss you when I'm gone."

It took just that long for her world to fracture and collapse. He wasn't planning to take her back to the States with him. He'd just told her so. Tactfully, kindly, but unmistakably.

The sound of her own voice amazed her. It didn't sound like someone who was fighting not to scream. "Not long now, is it?"

"Two weeks."

Not as much as that, she thought. One week and five days. She knew it by heart.

He rolled over and looked down at her. "We've had some great times, haven't we?"

"Wonderful, but—" she took her courage in her hands "—do they really need to end?"

The light was poor, but just enough for her to see the sudden tension in his face. She hastened to add, "I mean—you could get an extension."

"Oh, that. No, my time is up and your Immigration Department won't extend it. I did ask. No dice."

So he wanted to stay with her, she thought, clutching at straws. There was still time for him to ask her to go with him. But the time slipped by without a word, and suddenly it was the last day, and his plane was leaving at noon.

She went with him to the airport, and they sat sipping coffee while they waited for his call. There was a pain in the middle of her chest, like a heavy stone, and she didn't know how it was possible to endure that pain and keep smiling, but somehow it was. He was going, and he was happy about it. She didn't have to ask to know that his heart wasn't breaking. His thoughts had already leaped ahead to California.

She went with him to the gate, and at the last minute he threw his arms about her in a bear hug. "I'll never forget you, Pippa."

"Yes, you will," she said merrily. "There'll be some beauty in the next seat. You'll take one look at her and I'll vanish."

Deny it! Please deny it!

"Wretch!" he said, tweaking her nose. "That's what you think of me, is it?"

"This is the last call for—"

"That's it! Gotta go! Bye, baby. Be happy."

One last peck on her cheek and he was gone. Pippa watched him walking jauntily away, and although he turned for a final wave, she knew that she had already passed out of his life.

She forced herself to leave at once. She would not, *would* not become one of those pathetic creatures who stared at a space long after it was empty, as though expecting the person to reappear. Luke wouldn't turn back. She knew that. And she had too much pride to hang on hopelessly.

Sitting on the subway train on the journey home, she actually cheered up. She had always known this would happen, Luke had never made any secret of his departure date or the fact that there was no room for permanence in his life. They were both modern, liberated people who'd enjoyed a fling and would now get on with their lives.

She was pleasantly surprised to find herself coping so well. She smiled as she entered the guest house, stopped for a chat with Ma and went jauntily on to her room. Once, their room, now hers alone.

Alone.

The word was like the tolling of a bell, and it caught her off guard, just when she thought she was managing nicely. The smiles, the jauntiness and the bravery fell away as swiftly as discarded clothes, leaving her cold and trembling with shock. It was as much as she could do to lock the door before sliding to the floor in an agony of weeping.

He was gone, and she would never see him again.

Grief washed over her in endless waves, each one bigger than the first, until she buried her face in her hands to muffle her sobs. He was gone. He was gone.

For a week afterward she walked about like a zombie. She had no appetite and nearly made herself ill by working extra hours at her job, trying to wear herself out, without eating. So the first hint of pregnancy passed by without alerting her. By the time she was forced to recognize the truth she was nearly two months pregnant, and so tired and undernourished that she was actually losing weight. One evening she quietly fainted in Ma's kitchen. Sarah, one of the medical students, caught her as she fell. After that there was no longer any doubt.

She had the phone number of Luke's parents. Three times she started to telephone, and three times she aborted the call while it was still ringing. There was no way her pride would risk being answered by someone else, lamely explaining that she had known Luke in England, and was he there, please? She could see, as vividly as if they were in front of her, the significant glances his family would exchange.

One of Luke's passing fancies! Still fooling herself, poor thing!

And if he picked up the receiver himself? Hey, Luke...remember me? I'm Pippa—no, *Pippa!*

In the end she wrote to him, and it took four attempts to get exactly the tone of voice she wanted: pleased about the news, cheerful, not asking, demanding or even faintly expecting—"just thought you'd like to know."

She sent the letter off and began a week of agony, two weeks, three. Oh, God, he was going to ignore her! He probably felt entitled to. No strings. That had been the deal.

But she knew that if Luke, who was all the world to her, could brush her off in such a cheap, callous way, her heart would break forever.

After a month he telephoned, full of apologies. He'd been away from home, and his mail had just piled up. His voice was friendly, concerned, but not lover-like. In the joy of being able to believe in him again she found she could cope.

"How are you feeling?" he asked. "Queasy? Poor thing."

She actually managed to chuckle. "Luke, I never felt better in my life. It's no big deal."

"You're all right about it, then? I mean, you want to have the baby?"

"Of course. I'm looking forward to it."

"And it's okay—as things are? You don't feel the need of anything boring and old-fashioned...like a husband?"

"Luke, honestly! In this day and age?"

"Well, some people still do. Anyway, I'm available if—if you like."

So there it was. In his own, dutiful, roundabout way, he had asked her to marry him. The temptation to seize the chance was mind-blowing. Why not? Other men had started from this point and made happy marriages. She took a deep breath.

But before she could say the words, Luke added, "Of course, I'll support you and the baby whatever happens."

And the moment was gone. He'd spoken just quickly enough to tell her what answer he was hoping for. He was a nice boy and he had a conscience. But conscience wasn't enough.

"Darling, you're sweet, honestly you are," she said with a laugh. "But people don't have to get married these days. Am I such a weakling that I can't look after a little baby without you?"

"Just thought I might have a place in the proceedings, Ms. Modern and Liberated."

"Mr. Solid and Reliable," she teased. "You don't want to turn out like Frank, do you?"

"Perish the thought!"

They talked for a while longer, and he promised to send her some money soon. Laughing, she wished him all the best. She knew she'd done well, sounding just right, cheerful, invincible, ready to tackle life with a song.

Then she hung up.

Then she sat staring at the dead telephone.

Then she locked herself in her room and sobbed until there were no tears left in all the world.

When the rest of the boarding house heard about the coming baby, they took her under their various wings. Every budding doctor in the place regarded this pregnancy as his or her special province. She left the Ritz and became Ma's permanent cook. This was a relief to everyone. Luke's departure had been a blow to more than Pippa.

Josie's birth was treated as a house event, and the other mothers in the maternity ward looked on in envy as visitors crowded around Pippa's bed. They even took bets as to which of the five young men would turn out to be the father.

But none of them was. Josie's father sent a pretty

bouquet, a card with affectionate wording, and an extra check to "buy her something from me." But he didn't come to see her.

Soon after that, Ma's "rheumatics" grew worse, and Pippa took full-time control of the house. It was the perfect job for her, enabling her to keep Josie with her all the time, with an unlimited supply of willing baby-sitters. For this she received her room and board and enough money to enable her to bank the checks that came from Los Angeles.

Luke might be irresponsible in many ways, but as far as money went, he had never let her down. When his finances improved, so did hers. Over the years her nest egg grew fast, banked in high interest accounts. By the time Ma was ready to retire, Pippa had enough for a deposit, and was able to get a mortgage and buy her out. Luke promptly sent an extra ten thousand dollars to pay for refurbishments.

The place thrived. Pippa could now consider herself a successful businesswoman. Customers poured in, attracted by her high reputation and the excellence of her cooking. She thought wryly that she'd found herself in the same trap as her mother, longing to go wild with imaginative dishes, but catering for those who only wanted "good, plain food."

Sometimes she remembered her dream, to be the greatest cook in the world. But that dream seemed very far away now. As far away as Luke himself.

It was eleven years since she'd seen him, although his fast-growing celebrity status meant that she knew what he looked like. He'd grown a little heavier from the lean boy she remembered. He was a man now, but his face was still full of wicked humor and more attractive than any man had the right. The sight of his picture could still make her smile.

The pain had gone, leaving only sweet memories and Josie, a child to delight any mother's heart. On the whole it was a reasonably happy life, until one day, Jake, who'd just passed his medical exams, said, "Pip, for a woman in her twenties you get breathless far too quickly."

And suddenly she was a child again, saying, "Mummy, why are you always out of breath?"

"It's nothing, darling. Nothing at all."

But three months later her mother had been dead.

"It's nothing, Jake."

"You're telling *me?*" he'd demanded with gruff, angry affection. "When did you go to medical school? What does your doctor say?"

"Well, I haven't actually—"

"Then do it!"

So she had. And what the doctor had told her had been enough to put her on a plane to Los Angeles, to introduce Josie to her father while there was still time.

They were back at Luke's house in half an hour with the bags. Pippa got to work unpacking, "helped" by Josie, who bounced around getting underfoot until Pippa shooed her out.

"Go and talk to Daddy," she said brightly.

She kept the smile on her face until Josie had vanished, then sat down suddenly. Behind the laughter, she'd been desperate to send the child away before her gasps for breath became too noticeable. Josie knew only that her mother was occasionally poorly. She had no idea of the severity of her condition, and Pippa wanted to keep it that way until this trip was over. She clutched the end of the brass bedstead while her head swam.

"Not yet," she prayed frantically. *"A week. Just give me a week."*

Think about something else. Concentrate hard until it passes. Look around you. See how inviting this room is with its polished wood floor and two brass bedsteads, draped in white. No, don't look at the bed. It'll make you think how much you long to lie down. That's it. You're feeling better now.

Outside, on the balcony, she could hear Josie calling, "Mummy, look! We're at the seaside."

Until now Josie had been too preoccupied with meeting her father to have much attention for the scenery, but the full glory of her situation had burst on her all at once.

Luke joined her on the balcony. "Seaside!" he echoed with mock indignation. "That's more than just seaside."

Pippa made her way out to join them. Luke greeted her with a grin. "Your mom took me to a seaside resort in England once," he told Josie.

"And you said 'You don't call this a beach, do you?'" Pippa reminded him. "'*I* grew up on a real beach.'"

"And you said, 'Whadda ya mean, "a real beach"?'"

"*This* is a real beach," Josie said ecstatically. "No pebbles, just miles and miles of sand. Can we go and see it now?"

"Not now," Pippa said quickly. She could feel her strength running out by the minute.

"Oh *please*, Mummy."

"What about jet lag after that long flight?" Luke asked.

"I haven't got jet lag, honestly, I haven't," Josie insisted.

"But your mom has. She's an old lady and she needs her rest." He grinned at Pippa. "You do look done in. Go and crash while I take Josie to the beach."

There was nothing she wanted so much. She returned to their room and made a conscientious effort to finish the unpacking, but suddenly weariness came over her like a wave and she lay down thankfully on the bed.

She was aware of Luke slipping into the room and drawing the curtains against the light. He neared the bed, and his footsteps paused for a long moment, as though he'd stopped to gaze at her, then he left the room. As she heard the door close behind him, Pippa's mind was beginning the slide into blissful sleep, trying not to heed the thoughts that reached out to snag her on the way.

What will you do when you can't use jet lag as an excuse? You're a young woman and you move like an old one...always out of breath...always needing an excuse to lie down...what about when the pain comes? Dear God, let this go well! Josie is going to need her father so much.... Don't let them suspect before I'm ready to tell them....

Luke enjoyed nothing better than an excuse to visit the beach. He and Josie were gone for three hours, and by the time they returned home, father and daughter were thoroughly pleased with each other. As they approached the back door Luke was laughing at some idiotic remark of the child's, when Josie put a finger theatrically to her lips.

"Don't wake Mummy," she said.

"Think she'll still be asleep?"

"Mummy gets tired a lot. She's always napping during the day, 'cuz there's so much to do for the boarders."

"Well she's not going to work while she's here. We'll spoil her. Why don't you go and have a shower while I rustle up something to eat?"

Josie skipped off into the bedroom, but Luke saw her emerge a moment later, clutching some clothes, her finger to her lips.

"She still asleep?" he asked, and received a vigorous nod.

Luke went quietly past her and up to the bed. Pippa was lying on her face, one arm hanging over the edge, in exactly the same position as when he'd left her three hours ago. Sleeping like the dead.

Which was strange, because Pippa had never slept like that.

She was a compulsive twitcher. He remembered one particular time years ago when she'd asked, "Luke, what are you doing on the floor?"

"I spent the entire night on the floor. It was more comfortable that way, you mad woman."

"Meaning? *Meaning?*"

"Meaning that being with you is like trying to sleep with a flailing windmill. You punched me in the eye once, and where your knee landed I'd rather not think of."

"Oh, darling, I'm so sorry."

"Don't be sorry. Just keep your knees to your-self," he remembered saying.

Josie came into the kitchen while Luke was just about to dish up an egg concoction. She was wear-ing jeans and a shirt and shining from the shower.

"Coming up!" he exclaimed, heading for the place at the bar that he'd laid for her.

But Josie seemed not to hear him. She was gazing at the picture of Pippa and herself, standing in its place of honor. Luke put the plate down slowly. He'd seen the blissful smile on her face and knew he would need to tread very carefully for the next few minutes.

"What are you thinking?" he asked gently.

"Is it—here *all* the time?"

For a crazy instant he toyed with a fantasy in which the picture was always on show to an admir-ing world. It was so easy to say what women wanted to hear, and he'd never thought twice about it be-fore.

Except once, years ago, with a girl whose honesty brooked no compromise, and who'd made him hon-est, too—at least for a while. It hadn't been anything she said, just the look in her deep brown eyes, al-ways expecting the best from him. The same eyes in another face were watching him trustfully now.

"No," he admitted. "You and Mommy have been my special secret."

"Mummy said—" Josie didn't seem to know how to go on.

"What did she say?"

"She said she knew you loved us but—"

"Yes?"

"But you had another life, and we weren't part of it."

For once Luke was stuck for something to say.

"She said you knew lots of other people now, and maybe they didn't know about us and—"

He thought fast. "You were too precious to share. I've kept you for myself."

Josie smiled and seemed satisfied. She didn't know that she'd done what no other woman had ever managed: made Luke totally and thoroughly ashamed of himself. He recovered, but only with an effort.

"Why don't we get this eaten, while it's still good?" he said. "I'll make some more for Mommy when she's awake."

The little girl frowned. "Why do you say Mommy? It's Mummy."

"It's Mummy in England. Over here it's Mommy."

Josie frowned. "But Mommy's wrong. It's Mummy."

He set his chin. "Mommy!"

She set hers. "Mummy!"

"*Mommy!*"

"*Mummy!*"

"Oh, boy, are you ever her kid! Stubborn, argumentative—"

"What's argu—?"

"It means that nobody else ever gets the last word. She was just like that."

And about the damnedest things, he remembered:

"Pippa, what are you doing on the floor?" Luke had asked, the night following his sleep on the floor.

want it now.'' He began touching her with little tick-ling movements that sent sensation flowing over her skin. He was a devil who knew she couldn't hold out when she did that.

"What about that book?'' she demanded, feeling herself drowning in sensation. "Foreplay, and all that.''

"I've gone on to the next chapter,'' he said cheekily.

"Well I—haven't.'' Putting out all her strength she tossed him onto his back. He was surprised enough to let her win, and lay watching her out of glinting eyes that held a warning. He would enjoy her teasing, but he was far from tame. His proud, upstanding member proclaimed that.

She lightly touched the part of him she wanted most, thinking blissfully ahead but heightening the pleasure by deferring it. By now she knew how steely was Luke's control. He was ready, but he could stay ready for a long time. It was a kind of mutual teasing that they had perfected, and it thrilled her to know that she could excite him that much. Her fingers moved again, caressing and enjoying, loving the feel of him in her hand.

"You're playing with fire,'' he murmured.

"I know. That's how I like it best.''

"*Now,* Pippa.''

"Not...quite...now. *Hey!*'' For he had returned the compliment, tossing her onto her back and com-ing over her swiftly.

"I said now,'' he told her firmly against her mouth. "Unless you want to dispute the point.''

"Mmm. What point was that?''

Thought was becoming impossible as she felt him

giving her the slow, significant smile she loved. "Why don't you tell me about these other things?"

"Aren't you going to give me any help?"

"Nope. I'm just going to lie here and let you have your wicked way with me." He yawned provocatively. "I may even fall asleep."

"Over my dead body! Or yours!"

He grinned. "Woman, are you going to seduce me, or are you going to sit there and yak all night?"

"I'm going to seduce you," she whispered. "But first I'm going to enjoy just looking at you."

She drew back and feasted her eyes on him. Luke's shoulders weren't broad or heavy with muscles, and his strength was of the whipcord variety, so apart from his height he wasn't physically splendid: not if you were only looking. But Pippa wasn't only looking. She was remembering, too, and her memories were delicious.

"You're a shameless woman," he murmured.

"I know," she said as she trailed her hand over his smooth chest. "It's more fun that way. Don't you think?"

"If you put it like that," he said, speaking with difficulty, "then yes."

She chuckled and began to kiss him, his mouth first, then his neck, little tickling kisses that drew a growl from his throat. His hands began to go into action, but she stopped them.

"*I'm* supposed to be seducing *you,* remember?"

"Well, you've seduced me now," he said, grinning. "Let's get on to the next bit."

"Wait," she said, fending him off. "Learn to be patient."

"To hell with that. If it's worth waiting for, I

They reminded her of a couple of dormice, not exciting, but cosy and content together.

Near the end of the reception Elly took Pippa aside and said, archly, "Such a very handsome young man! When will we hear wedding bells for you?"

"You won't," Pippa said. To her relief Luke was on the other side of the room swapping funny stories with the best man.

"But anyone can see you two are crazy about each other," Elly protested.

Pippa discovered that she didn't have her heart under such perfect control as she'd hoped, otherwise the suggestion that Luke was crazy about her wouldn't have made it leap like that. But she assumed a worldly-wise air.

"I'm eighteen. I've got a lot of road to travel before I'm ready to settle down."

"You mean he hasn't asked you?"

"I mean that every little fling doesn't have to end in marriage these days. Neither Luke or I care about doing the conventional thing. Elly, honestly, I'm really happy for you and Frank. I think you're perfect together. But things are different for my generation."

To which Elly simply replied, "Hmm!" with a look of disconcerting shrewdness in her baby-blue eyes.

Frank and Luke talked for a conscientious ten minutes, but both were relieved when it was over. Frank was kind and well-meaning, but he was also pompous and narrow-minded, and before she left he said firmly to Pippa, "That young man isn't at all suitable for you, my dear. I'm afraid I'd have to call him rackety.''

"He's twenty-three," Pippa said incensed. "Weren't you rackety when you were his age?"

He was shocked. "Certainly not!"

"Well, you should have been! Everyone should be rackety at twenty-three. He's got years and years to be responsible."

"You sound as though you're quoting him," Frank said, scoring a bull's-eye and momentarily throwing her off balance. "Don't give him your heart, Pippa. He'll only break it."

She tried to sound nonchalant. "Maybe I'll break his."

"I hope so. But I'm afraid the world doesn't work that way."

"Oh, Frank, don't be so stuffy! I'm having a wonderful time with Luke. Who cares about tomorrow?" She flitted away before he could say any more. She couldn't cope with Frank's disconcerting insights.

As they lay in each other's arms that night, Luke kissed her and said, "I'm afraid Frank and I bring out the worst in each other."

"I know. He said you were rackety. I told him he should have been rackety at your age."

Luke shouted with laughter. "I wish I could have seen his face. It's not his way, any more than pipe and slippers are mine."

"Who wants pipe and slippers?" she murmured, beginning to nibble him. "There are other things…"

"Mmm?" He lay back and stretched luxuriously, one arm behind his head, one leg carelessly raised,

"You didn't talk like that last time. Roses? You?"

"I'd have bought you roses if I'd had any money. I just never did."

"No, we didn't have two pennies to rub together, did we?"

"And we didn't care," he said slowly.

"No, we didn't care."

She stretched again as luxuriously as a cat. Luke regarded her, marveling that she still had the same figure that he recalled, slender, lithe and flexible. Memories were coming back to him, how pert and saucily elegant she'd been when she was naked, and how filled with acrobatic energy. Exhausting, and how! Why, he remembered—

He wondered self-consciously if she could read his thoughts in his face, but she was lying full-out with her eyes closed and a contented smile on her face. With an effort he clothed the naked vision. Clothes, that was it. Think of clothes quickly. She could always carry off the most outrageous garments.

That's what was different, he realized. She was wearing slacks and sweater that were pleasant enough, even attractive, but not designed to be eye-catching.

He got up suddenly. "I'll be back."

He vanished, and a few moments later she heard a "ping" from the telephone extension on a low table beside her. She could just make out the murmur of Luke's voice from the kitchen. He was gone about ten minutes.

"I had to make some calls to clear the time for you and Josie," he said. "The only thing I couldn't cancel was recording the show. You might like to come and see that.''

''Mmm, lovely. Josie will be thrilled to be in a TV studio.''

''But you won't want to sit there for two solid days. Why don't you take a shopping trip on the second day—my treat? Go to Rodeo Drive and buy yourself and Josie some knock-out clothes.''

''Luke, even I've heard of Rodeo Drive and what it costs to shop there.''

''I told you, it's my treat. You take my card and buy anything you want.''

Pippa was silent for a moment, then she sat up. She was looking at him in a way that worried him, although he couldn't think why.

''This wouldn't be your gold card you're offering me, would it Luke?'' And there was no doubt about it, he thought. Her voice was definitely unfriendly.

''Yes, it would, if that matters.''

''The one you gave Dominique, no doubt?''

''Well—yes.''

''Fine. That's what gold cards are for—popsies. Dominique is a popsie. I'm the mother of your child. There's a big difference.''

Silence. Then he drew a long, careful breath. ''Oh, boy! I really screwed up, didn't I?''

She relented. ''Just a little. Sorry, I didn't mean to get heavy, but it just didn't feel right.''

''What about Josie? Can't I buy her some pretty dresses?''

''Josie hates pretty dresses. She thinks they're for wimps. She wears jeans with sweaters, jeans with jackets, jeans with T-shirts. Since it's so hot here

"I'm trying to go to sleep."

"Then get into the bed. *I'm* sleeping on the floor."

"You slept on the floor last night. And according to you, it was all my fault. You said I was twitching, which was a black lie—"

"I said you kneed me in the groin, and I have the bruises to prove it. Don't expect any action from me tonight."

"So sleep well and recover, *fast!*"

"Think I'm a ninety-eight pound weakling, huh? Pippa, get into that bed."

"Nope. I'm sleeping on the floor."

"So am I."

"And so am I!"

"We can't both sleep on the damned floor!"

"Right! G'night Luke! I'm sleeping here. So off you go!"

"Pippa, stop that, y'hear me? I'm ticklish. No, stop it. Gerroff! *Now* will you stop?"

"Thought you were out of action tonight."

"Guess I'm not so bad as I thought."

"Mmm!"

A while later he asked, "Wouldn't it have been more comfortable in bed?"

"Let's find out."

"Daddy?"

"Sorry, honey. What?"

"You went into a trance with a funny smile on your face."

"I was just remembering one time—we had the craziest arguments—she just had to be the one who slept on the floor—guess I talked her out of that."

He saw his daughter giving him a puzzled look and said hastily, "Eat your supper." He poured her a glass of orange juice and re-angled the picture.

"Why do you keep a computer in the kitchen?" she asked.

"Because this is where I live. It's the center of my life."

Pippa's head appeared around the door. She was wearing one of Luke's capacious white bathrobes over her nightdress, and had obviously just gotten out of bed. But her eyes were bright, and she looked well. In fact, she looked like the old vigorous Pippa, and he could shrug aside the stillness that had worried him while she slept.

He came to stand in front of her, grinning. She grinned back, and the next moment they were in each other's arms, laughing, bear hugging with pleasure.

"Oh, boy, is it good to see you!" he yelled. "Pippa! My Pippa, after all this time. Let me look at you." He held her away. "Still as ugly as ever, I see. *Yuk!*"

"Yuk yourself! What any woman ever saw in you I can't imagine. You were bad enough then, but now you're a disaster. Fat—balding—"

"And you should see my dandruff!" he agreed.

They exploded into laughter again, hugging each other and dancing around the kitchen. Josie watched them with glee, cramming her mouth full, and chuckling between bites.

"Sit down and have some supper," he said, pointing her to a bar stool.

"Can I just have some coffee now and come back when I've had a shower?"

"Your wish is my command. Fresh coffee coming up."

She took the cup he offered and turned to leave, but Josie forestalled her, calling, "Mummy, did you know that while we're here, you're Mommy?"

"I had a feeling I might be." She smiled at Josie. "Mommy it is."

"Come and sit down," Josie commanded.

"Well, I—" Pippa slipped a hand into the pocket of the bathrobe and fingered the pills that she must take very soon.

"I want to tell you all about the beach," Josie persisted.

"Just a moment, then I must go and have a shower." She sat down at the bar beside her daughter, who launched into a vigorous description of the last few hours, which had obviously been pure heaven to her. Pippa listened contentedly. This was exactly what she'd hoped for when she came here. All would be well.

"What's that you're taking?" Luke asked, seeing her slip something into her mouth.

"Just an aspirin," she said quickly. "Bit of a headache."

A wise look came over Josie's face, aging her several years. "Have you got another one of your headaches?" she asked kindly. To Luke she explained, "She's always getting them."

"Darling, don't exaggerate. I get tired with so much work to do in that stuffy boarding house, and today's been a long day." Pippa laughed. "I don't know why I'm having a shower as though it was breakfast time, when it's actually evening."

"It'll make you feel better," Luke said. "Wash the cobwebs away."

He was right. After a shower she felt like a new woman. She dressed hurriedly and returned to the kitchen, where Josie was trying to decide on the rival merits of toffee or banana ice cream, and finally honoring them both with her approval.

"You've cleaned both plates," Luke declared, as though astonished.

"She's ten," Pippa reminded him. "What did you expect?"

Josie opened her mouth to say something, but no sound came out. She had been up for twenty-four hours, and before their eyes jet lag overcame her like a cloud. Her eyes closed, her head fell forward, and she would have fallen off the bar stool had Luke not caught her in his arms.

They went up in procession to the bedroom, where Luke deposited the little girl on the bed. "Leave her as she is," he said, pulling the coverlet over her. "She doesn't want to be bothered with getting undressed now."

"Night, Mommy," Josie murmured with her eyes closed.

"Night, darling." Pippa bent and kissed her.

"Night, Daddy."

"Night, sweetheart." He leaned down and kissed the child quite naturally, without a hint of the awkwardness many men would have felt.

That was Luke, Pippa remembered: easy, tactile, uninhibited, the warmth and charm always available on tap—as long as they weren't crushed by too many expectations.

He gave her another delightful demonstration a moment later as they returned to the kitchen.

"And now, eef Madame would care to be seated," he declared in a horrible stage French accent, "zis establishment will provide eggs by Luke of ze Ritz."

"You remembered how I like them?" she exclaimed, astonished.

"Of course. I created this especially for you. Don't you remember?"

It was a brilliantly simple invention consisting of poached eggs and avocado, with a sauce Pippa had never been able to analyze. It was her first taste of it for nearly eleven years, and it was delicious.

"Just for me," she echoed.

"I have to admit that I put it in the restaurants—"

"So I should jolly well hope! Is it a success?"

"The greatest. But it was always really for you."

She looked into his smiling eyes and thought, I'm so glad that I'm not in love with you anymore. If I were, you could still devastate me. Lucky for me I'm wiser now.

He made fresh coffee, and drank some with her, watching her fondly like a recovered treasure.

"What happened to Luke of the Ritz," she asked smiling, "after he got back home?"

"Oh, he drifted around from one job to another."

"Don't tell me he had trouble finding work? Not the genius I remember?"

"Work of a sort, but not the sort I wanted. Always having to scale my ideas down to someone else's guidelines, never allowed to do things my way.

"I used to pour out my frustrations to an old fellow I met on the beach. His name was Tommy, and he had a dog, called Catch, the fattest spaniel you ever saw. I guess I just naturally gravitate to beach bums, being half one myself—my mom would tell you that—but Tommy and Catch became my best friends for a while.

"I used to take them both back to my rooms, practice recipes on them, and we'd talk for hours. I visited him once at his home. He had a little place, but he didn't spend much time there because it was too far from the beach. If you've finished eating, let's go into the other room. It's more comfortable.''

Chapter Five

They ferried the coffeepot into the large room where he lived when he wasn't working. One wall was a huge window, overlooking the sea. Sofas and armchairs looked as though they'd been thrown down casually.

"Here," Luke said, settling her on a sofa directly in front of the window. "Coffee's on the table beside you."

It was lovely to be waited on. Pippa kicked off her shoes and stretched out on the sofa. "Mmm!" she sighed.

He laughed and settled into an armchair where he could see her face. "Where was I?"

"Tommy and Catch."

"Right. Tommy shouldn't have been living on his own, but his only relative was a daughter he didn't get on with. She said he could stay with her if he had the dog put down. Said he was vicious, which was a damned lie because he was too fat to be vicious. So Tommy went on living alone, except for Catch, who was all he had to love.

"Then Tommy died suddenly, and left a will, saying everything he had was mine, if I'd look after Catch. So I took him home, put him on a diet, and he lived another three years. But here's the incredible thing. It turned out Tommy owned the place where he lived. He'd bought it fifty years ago before prices had shot through the roof, and I'm not sure he ever realized what it was worth.

"That was when the daughter reappeared, screaming blue murder, saying how I'd influenced the old man and stolen her inheritance."

"What did you do?" Pippa asked, genuinely curious to know how Luke's sweet temper would have dealt with this one.

"I'd have cheerfully fought her to the end. She was mean to Tommy, and everyone knew it, but she was miserable and lonely, and I reckoned money was all she was ever going to have, so I offered her a third and her lawyer advised her to settle.

"When the house was sold, that still left me enough to get started. I found a place that was already a restaurant but not doing as well as it should. Tommy's money paid just over half the purchase price, and a bank loan covered the rest including the cost of making it over how I wanted."

"And it was a huge success, and soon you had enough for the second restaurant," Pippa said triumphantly.

"Not quite. It was a success, but the money came in slowly, and banks are cautious. There was a moment when I just knew it was right to expand. There was a place for sale exactly where I wanted it, and the price was reasonable. I had one day to clinch it. Would the bank listen? No way.''

''Tightwads!''

''Right. If it wasn't for Claudia, I'd be sunk.''

''Who's Claudia?''

''Oil heiress. She owns a house a couple of hours from here, in Montecito, and she spends a month there every year. When she was in Los Angeles she would eat at Luke's Place, and we got to know each other. To make a long story short, she gave me the loan for Luke's Other Place, or I couldn't have bought it. Soon after that I got the TV spot, and now I'm well on the way to paying her back, with interest.''

Pippa chuckled. ''If there was one thing about you that used to get up my nose, it was the way you always fell on your feet.''

''That's true,'' he reflected. ''The cavalry always came galloping to the rescue, like you today, turning up just when Dominique was getting heavy.'' He became awkward suddenly. ''About Dominique—''

''Luke, you don't owe me any explanations. We went our separate ways years ago. You put the picture in a drawer and took it out when it was useful.''

Hearing it put that way, he winced. But there was no blame in Pippa's eyes. She knew him from way back and accepted him for what he was. He was the one who suddenly didn't like it.

''It was fate,'' he said. ''Fate knew you were coming at just the moment I needed you. Come to think of it, that's true.''

''Yes, what would you have done without us?''

she asked, amused. "You'd be halfway up the aisle by now."

He shuddered. "Please don't say things like that. It makes me feel queasy. From now on that picture's staying there all the time. And while you're here I'm going to take plenty more."

"That's nice."

"Just what did bring you here suddenly? And why didn't you let me know you were coming?"

"You know I always did crazy things on the spur of the moment," Pippa said with a shrug. "The guest house is doing well and I took on an assistant. Susan's bright enough to be left in charge. One of my boarders can get cheap airline tickets, and I thought—why not?"

She was quite pleased with the speech. It had just the right air of daft spontaneity, and who would guess how long she'd rehearsed it?

"Besides," she went on with her other prepared speech, "I needed a break. I've been having a load of minor ailments recently. I get migraines, and sometimes asthma, and the doctor says I've got a touch of anemia."

"That's terrible," he said, taking her hand. "You were always so full of beans."

"Well, I still am, basically. I just live on iron pills, and I'm better than I was. It's only little things. Not life threatening."

Not life threatening. Not like the heart condition that she ought to be at home being treated for this minute.

"But I get a bit short of energy," she finished cheerfully, "so sometimes it'll be just you and Josie doing things without me."

"Whatever you say. You do exactly what you want to."

"Well, I thought a holiday would do me good. So here we are."

"And I'm going to love having you, but you were crazy not to warn me. Suppose I hadn't been at home? I'd have missed you."

"No, we'll be here for about a week, and I know your show goes out twice a week, so we were bound to overlap."

"But we weren't. I record those shows six at a time. In between I can be away for as much as ten days."

"I never thought of that," she said, horrified.

"I wouldn't have wanted to miss Josie for anything. We're already on the same wavelength."

"She's the perfect age to appreciate you," Pippa agreed.

"Is that your way of telling me I have the mental age of a ten year old?"

"What do you think?"

"I think I'll fetch some wine," he said hastily, and vanished back into the kitchen.

The sun was setting over the ocean, a vast, magnificent sight that made her go to the window and stand, almost breathless with the beauty of it. "I can see why you bought a house in just this spot," she said, hearing Luke enter behind her. "Imagine having this, all the time."

"All the time," he agreed, coming up behind her and putting his hands on her shoulders. "I'm so glad I had the chance to show it to you. And I've got you both for a whole week. I'm going to make this the best vacation you've ever had."

"As long as Josie enjoys herself, and you and she get to know each other."

"What about you and me?"

"We already do know each other," she said with a smile.

"That was then. This is now."

Still standing behind her, he slipped his arms right around her, crossing them in front, and gave her a friendly little hug. It was the kind of thing Luke did easily without it meaning anything. She could see the two of them reflected in the dark window, their faces side by side.

You're weakening, said the warning voice. Any moment you're going to succumb to his charm. And you promised yourself not to.

She moved, turning in the circle of his arms just enough to make him break his hold. "Can I have some more of that wine?"

"Sure. Sit down," he said cheerfully.

He filled her glass and asked, "How are things back home, your family and so on?"

"My father died five years ago. We hadn't seen much of each other. I took Josie to see him but it wasn't a success, and he and I had nothing to say to each other. Clarice remarried fairly soon after his death. What about your parents?"

"They're going strong, still living in Manhattan. Like Tommy, they bought their house before the property prices shot through the roof. My brother Zak and sister Becky are both earning more than Dad ever did, but they can't afford to buy around here so they're still living at home. What about Frank and Elly? Did they have that crowd of kids they wanted?"

"Not even one, I'm afraid. And they haven't had any luck adopting. The highlight of their lives is when I take Josie to visit."

"Poor little soul."

"They adore her, and they're very kind people."

"I believe you. It's just that I can't imagine a worse fate for a kid than having Frank as a father."

"Josie's very fond of him. But I must admit she finds him a bit slow."

"Slow, boring, narrow-minded, pompous…"

"All right, all right," she laughed. "He admires you, too."

"Rackety, he said I was, didn't he?"

"Yes, well, he knew one when he saw one."

"Thanks. You always knew how to give it to me right between the eyes."

"I saw through you and out the other side."

"Not always. I pulled a few fast ones that you knew nothing about."

Something stabbed at her heart. He was going to say he'd been seeing another girl all those years ago. But how? He'd spent every moment with her.

"So tell me about these fast ones you pulled?" she said as casually as she could. "Had a whole harem I didn't know about, did you? The Romeo of the Ritz we used to call you. Girl on each floor."

"It's nothing like that. I might be many kinds of a jerk, Pippa, but I wasn't that kind of a jerk." He added conscientiously, "Not with you, anyway. While we were together, you were the only one."

Her heart stilled its unruly beating, but she was shocked at herself for the fierceness of her relief. It shouldn't have mattered. But it had mattered terribly.

He went on. "But I had other little angles that you knew nothing about."

"Oh, yeah?" she said in the old way.

"Oh, yeah!"

She leaned toward him. *"Oh, yeah?"*

He leaned to her. *"Oh, yeah!"*

"OH, YEAH?"

"OH, YEAH!"

They burst out laughing together, and she fell back on the sofa, stretching out luxuriously. It was comfortable, the brandy was good, and she was beginning to relax.

"That was almost the first thing we said to each other," he said. "Remember?"

"I remember you turning up in Green Park to find me missing, throwing up your hands to the skies and crying, 'Please, please, no!'"

"You imagined that!"

"No way!" she teased. "You were really desperate at the thought that I might not be there."

"Yes, I was," he said unexpectedly. "It mattered. But then you came back—because of course you found me irresistible—"

"Oh, really?"

"So I took pity on you—" He saw her eyeing him balefully, and his expression became suddenly rueful. "If you hadn't come back I was going to turn the Ritz inside out looking for you. And then I was going to go on my knees asking forgiveness, offering you a big bunch of roses—*now what?*"

"I'm sorry, Luke," she choked. "But I can't keep a straight face when you talk like that."

"You fell for it last time," he said aggrieved.

with her, like parents should be, so it ought to be simple, right?

Wrong!

Wrong because she brought memories of the sexiest time of your life, memories that made you horny just to think of them. Yet now she was like a different woman, with all the mystery of unexplored territory. And the mixture of the new and the familiar was driving you crazy.

But she solved the problem by yawning and heading for the door, pausing only to give your hand a squeeze—a *squeeze,* for Pete's sake! The last time a girl squeezed your hand you'd been on the back porch, with Mom breathing loudly behind the kitchen door, just in case you thought you were going to get away with anything. You didn't then, and you knew you weren't going to now.

So you played it cool, jumping to your feet and saying heartily, "Right, right. Big day tomorrow. Need plenty of sleep."

Then you realized you were babbling and made yourself shut up.

Just to turn the knife a little she looked back to smile, and there was something in that smile you'd never seen before, a shadowed quality, that only made her more mysterious. When she went on to her room, you stayed where you were, not daring to move until the silence told you she'd gone to bed.

And then you went and had a cold, cold shower.

In the early hours of the morning Pippa crept into the front room. The curtains were drawn back from the huge window so that she had a glorious view of the ocean, almost still in the dawn light. She sat

of money lay on her like a glow. Suddenly Pippa's clothes felt as though she'd rescued them from a garbage dump.

"Hello," said the vision. "I'm Claudia," she said. "Is Luke here?"

"No, he's on the beach," Pippa said, standing back to let her enter. "I'm Pippa Davis."

Claudia enveloped Pippa in a scented embrace. "I've been longing to meet you. Everyone's talking about you."

She didn't define *everyone*. This wasn't the moment for Claudia to mention Dominique, who'd called her with a garbled tale of a schemer who'd gotten her claws into Luke.

The child isn't even his, the model had wailed. *Anyone can see that, but poor Luke is completely taken in.*

And Claudia had said, *Don't be a fool, Dominique. Luke never does anything that doesn't suit Luke. I adore him, but I'm wise to him.*

"Talking about me?" Pippa echoed.

"You and Josie. Is she on the beach with him?"

"Yes, he's teaching her to bodysurf." Pippa was filled with a sinking dismay. This wasn't a vulgar popsie like Dominique. This was oil wells and Cartier and class and utter self-confidence.

"I thought he might turn out to be on the beach," Claudia said, pulling at the buttons of her simple blue linen dress. "So I came prepared." She tossed the dress aside, revealing a black one-piece. "Come on, let's go and join them."

That was what money did for you, made it possible for you to walk in on a stranger, scoop them up and take them swimming. Protests died on

Pippa's lips, and before she knew it, she'd donned her own costume and was crossing the road with Claudia.

Her dark-crimson one-piece was beautiful against her hair and warm skin, but against the glorious Claudia she felt like a dowdy schoolgirl. Then she forgot to be self-conscious in the pleasure of seeing Josie shrieking with excitement as her father taught her the secrets of riding the big waves that came rolling onto the beach. She had obviously taken to it, because Pippa could hear her cry, "Again, Daddy, again!" And Luke grinned, proud of her style and intrepidity.

"Is that your daughter?" Claudia asked, her eyes on them.

"Yes—and Luke's," Pippa replied.

At that moment Luke spotted them and came bounding out of the surf, Josie's hand clasped in his. He enveloped Claudia in an exuberant hug, unself-consciously pulling her against his bare, glistening torso. Pippa braced herself for a similar greeting, but he only smiled at her and nodded. Which was fine, she told herself.

Josie spoke politely to Claudia, but then grabbed Pippa's hand, pleading, "Mommy, come into the water."

"All right, darling." Laughing, she allowed herself to be dragged down the beach.

Luke would have followed, but Claudia laid a hand on his arm. "Luke, she's a great kid, but are you sure she's yours?"

"You've been talking to Dominique," he said, still looking out to sea where Pippa and Josie were splashing each other and laughing.

"Maybe I have," Claudia persisted, "but it's still a fair question."

"Not to me. Dominique is suspicious because she's only just heard about Josie. But I've known from the start. Pippa called me when she knew she was pregnant, and we've stayed in touch all this time."

"That still doesn't prove Josie is yours."

"Okay, for one thing there's the timing. She was conceived while Pippa and I were living together, and Pippa sure as hell wasn't seeing anyone else, not the way we—" he coughed and reddened "—never mind. That's not the real reason."

"So what is?"

"Pippa. The kind of person she is. There's nobody more honest. It made her special. She even made me honest for a while."

"You?"

"Yeah, hilarious isn't it? But we had something that—well, anyway, if she says it's true, it's true."

"And now she's turned up, after all these years?"

"She wanted me to meet Josie, and she was right. I left it too long."

"Sure she hasn't come back for you?"

"Well if she has, she's going about it a damned funny way," he growled. "Last night I got warned off—at least, I think so. It was hard to tell, but it sure wasn't a come-on."

"Darling, that's the oldest trick in the book. She'd have been very silly to throw herself straight into your arms."

"No," he growled. "I told you she isn't like that. *Hell!*"

A large wave had swooped out of nowhere and

knocked Josie and Pippa off their feet. As they floundered to pick themselves up, Luke was racing down the beach, plunging into the water, picking them up, asking urgent questions.

Josie made large gestures, delighted with the experience and trying to describe it to her father. Pippa was laughing as she wrung the water out of her hair. For a moment the dazzling sun threw the three of them into silhouette like figures on a frieze. Then another big wave came, causing Luke to move instinctively to shield the other two. Claudia watched for a while before walking thoughtfully into the water to join them.

They spent the rest of the morning together, and when they parted it was agreed that Claudia would join them that evening at Luke's Other Place.

"I've got to be there tonight," Luke explained to Pippa, "because they're doing the cooking for tomorrow's shows. So we'll check out the kitchens, and you can tell me what you think."

"Until tonight, then," Claudia said, blew a kiss in the general direction of them, and hurried out to her car. As soon as she settled behind the wheel she dialed a number on her car phone.

"Dominique? I've just left Luke—yes, I've met her, and the child, and I'm very glad you called me. Certainly something needs to be done, and the sooner the better. Be at Luke's Other Place this evening, at nine o'clock—no, just leave the details to me."

Chapter Six

Luke's Other Place was halfway along Manhattan Avenue. His first restaurant was glamorous, upmarket and very expensive. This one was fun. The prices were reasonable, the range of food wide, with a strong emphasis on Latin American because Luke loved it. Also he'd recently engaged Ramon, a Mexican genius whom he overpaid while skillfully picking his brains.

The decor suggested beach life. One whole wall was given up to a painting of Manhattan Beach Pier done by a local artist. Anyone sitting at one of the tables might think he'd dropped in to a picnic.

Behind the carefully rustic scenes, the kitchens were state-of-the-art, with flashing lights and buzzers on the gleaming ovens. Luke showed them all over, carefully explaining to Josie that each dish he would need next day was being cooked three times over, to three different stages. Josie nodded and asked some intelligent questions, which pleased her father to bursting point. Then she began to prowl around, asking more questions of the staff, who loved her.

"You did it," Pippa said to Luke. "Just as you said."

"I hoped you'd think so."

"Mind you, it's not exactly the Ritz, is it?"

He laughed "You should see the first restaurant."

They dined on Creole pasta, followed by fillet of salmon, grilled with ginger, lime and sesame glaze, which sent Josie into seventh heaven. She was even more thrilled at what was to come. Luke's Other Place was famous for its vast array of ice creams and toppings.

Pippa was happy for her, but her own feelings were more complicated. As she'd said to Luke, he'd done it. It was she who was still stranded in culinary mediocrity. Then she pulled herself together. As though it could matter now!

She became aware that Luke was staring at something, dismay all over his face. Following his gaze, she saw Dominique standing statuesquely in the entrance, dressed to kill, looking around her. Claudia promptly got to her feet and went to meet her, hands extended, smile blazing.

"What brought her here?" Luke muttered. "She never comes to this place, it's not grand enough for her."

Claudia was bringing Dominique ruthlessly over. The model gritted her teeth at the sight of Luke in the center of a family party. He grinned and blew her a kiss.

"Hi, honey. Glad you could make it here at last. I told you you'd love it. You know everyone, don't you?"

"We met yesterday," she said graciously.

"You're the lady without any clothes on," Josie declared innocently. She looked around the dumbstruck group. "Well, she was."

"Not quite," Luke said hastily. "Dominique, what can I get you?"

"Something fat-free," Dominique said faintly.

"You've come to the wrong place for that," Josie confided. "It's all crawling with calories and disgustingly delicious, isn't it, Daddy?"

"Hush brat, do you want to put me out of business?" he said with a grin.

"I'll have a salad and some mineral water," Dominique said austerely.

Luke summoned a waiter and relayed the order.

"Daddy," Josie said pathetically.

"I haven't forgotten you, honey." To Dominique he confided, "We were just about to study the ice cream question in great depth."

"Can we go back to the kitchen?" Josie asked eagerly.

"No need, here it is."

A huge circular trolley was being wheeled toward. It had five tiers, each adorned with tubs of ice cream and toppings.

"Yummy!" Josie and Claudia said with one voice.

Pippa, too, was fond of ice cream, and it developed into a three-way argument with Luke acting as referee. Dominique, dining on a puritanical salad and a virtuous mineral water, was left isolated and ridiculous—as perhaps Claudia had foreseen.

Josie regarded her with pity from behind a mountain of many flavored ice creams topped off with chocolate sauce that was truly "disgustingly delicious."

"Wouldn't you much rather have ice cream?" she asked. "It's ever so nice."

"No thank you," Dominique said. "I need to think of my figure."

"But you've got a smashing figure," Josie said generously.

"Thank you." Dominique relaxed a little.

"Do you have to work really, really hard at it?"

"That's enough, Josie," Luke said hastily. "Eat your ice cream before it melts."

"Any swaps for my pistachio?" Claudia enquired. "Josie, your raspberry looks delicious."

There was a general swapping, with long spoons moving back and forth and a lot of laughter. Then Pippa and Josie simultaneously made a takeover bid for Claudia's coffee and nut, and in the resulting melee a huge dollop landed on Luke's favorite pair of five-hundred-dollar slacks.

"Oh, dear," Pippa said. "I'm sorry."

"Sorry, Daddy," Josie said.

"Yes, it's a pity, isn't it?" he said ruefully. "A real waste of good ice cream."

Josie giggled.

"How about you?" Luke turned solicitously to Dominique, beside him. "Did any go over you?"

"Luckily, no," she said. "But I've just remembered an urgent appointment. Good night, everyone. It's been *so* nice." She rose, gave the barest nod of farewell and stalked away. Claudia followed at once, and before they reached the exit the others saw Dominique turn on her. They couldn't hear the words, but it was obvious that Dominique was in a sulphurous temper.

"You planned this whole thing," she spat at Claudia.

"I've done you a favor."

"You said something needed to be done—"

"And I've done it. On the beach this morning I saw a side of Luke I've never seen before. Now you've seen it, too, and I've saved you wasting any more time on a man you can't win. Luke's spoken for. I guess he's been spoken for for the last eleven years, even if nobody knew it, including Luke."

"That dowdy little nobody—"

"Wise up, Dominique. He *cares* about her. I saw that in the first five minutes. I don't know if he's in love with her, but he cares about her in a way that he doesn't care about anyone else, except Josie. One day you'll thank me."

"Well, don't hold your breath." Dominique swept out.

"Was it accident that she showed up tonight?" Luke demanded when Claudia returned to them.

"No," she said calmly. "I sent for her. It seemed only kind to make her face facts."

"Thanks," Luke muttered. "Guess you came to my rescue again."

"Someone always does, Luke," Claudia said tartly. "That's how you fix things. Someday you'll find yourself in a situation you can't fix."

Without waiting for his answer, she turned to Pippa and gave her a broad wink. Pippa had only

tions with Frank were always fraught because neither of them could say what was really in their mind.

Frank couldn't say, If you die I want Josie to fill
the place of the child Elly and I never had, and I'm
afraid of Luke in case he tries to claim her.

And Pippa couldn't say, You're a kind man but
limited. You'll teach Josie the sensible things, but I
want her to know the crazy ones, too—the things
that only her true father can teach her.

She smiled ruefully and went on in her head, talking perhaps to Frank and perhaps to herself.

He's not a solid, upright citizen. He's tricky, un-
reliable and unscrupulous. He does what suits him
and tap dances his way out of it afterward. But he's
warm and sweet, funny and charming, and he carries
magic with him wherever he goes. He's a taker and
a user, but he gives back so much that it works out
a fair bargain in the end.

The light was growing stronger over the sea. She
sat gazing at it, thrilled by the beauty of the sight.

I'm glad, she thought, yes, I really am glad that
I didn't make him marry me all those years ago.
Nature designed him to be a lover, not a husband.

She'd had a bad moment when she'd thought he
was about to admit to an old infidelity. She
shouldn't care now, but she did. Those few months
still lived as the brightest, loveliest time of her life.
Whatever the Luke of today was like, the Luke of
yesterday had been all hers. And if she had lost that
belief, her heart would have broken as cruelly today
as it would have done then.

She was awakened early by Josie, eager to be up
and doing. "Come on Mommy, Daddy says when

down by the phone, and called Frank in England. He answered so quickly that Pippa knew he'd been sitting by it.

"Just to let you know we landed safely," she said cheerfully.

"Does Luke know you're there?"

"Yes, he greeted us with open arms. Josie was thrilled."

"Pippa—"

"It's true, so you can take that disbelieving note out of your voice."

"The important thing is, how are you feeling?"

"Pretty good. The flight left me a bit tired—"

"You're lucky it didn't kill you. Do you realize what a state your heart's in?"

"Of course. The doctor laid it on the line. Why do you think I'm here? Because I know there are things I must do while there's time."

"And what happens if you collapse out there? Have you thought of Josie?"

"This is all for Josie's sake. It was important for Luke to know her."

"I don't see why. He's never taken any interest in her until now. You know Elly and I were against this trip, for your sake as much as hers."

"I can't talk now," Pippa said quickly. "Luke's coming back."

"Which hotel are you in?"

"We're staying with him."

There was a silence from the other end, before Frank said sharply, "I see. Goodbye."

Pippa hung up. She hadn't really heard Luke. She'd invented the excuse to end the call because she didn't want to go over old ground. Conversa-

half followed the conversation, but now she saw that Claudia's eyes were honest, humorous and shrewd. This woman was nobody's fool, she thought, beginning to like her.

Luke's show was recorded at the studios of GFI-Cable, on Marine Street. One show in the morning and two in the afternoon made a long day, and they set out very early next morning.

"Don't expect too much," he warned on the journey. "This isn't NBC or any of those big-time stations. We just work out of a cellar."

Ten minutes later he swung down into an underground parking lot, and they made their way to the studio, which Pippa thought was a good deal smarter than he'd made it sound, although far from grand. Josie seemed entranced by the cameras, the lights overhead and the people wandering around with clipboards. Best of all was the set, done up to look like a traditional kitchen with copper pans and glowing wooden doors. The walls were red. The work surfaces were red. The knobs and handles were brass. Remembering the clinical precision of Luke's real kitchens Pippa studied this rustic kitsch with amusement.

She'd always known that easygoing Luke could be a dictator, even a tyrant, where his work was concerned. But the years had developed him. On the journey to the studio he'd used his car phone to check that the food was on its way. The discovery that it wasn't brought forth a few crisp words that left no doubt of Luke's feelings. They reached the studio to find the van just ahead of them, already being unloaded by two of his employees. He bounded out of the car and gave them a stream of instructions, ending with, "And don't start the microwave until I tell you."

They wouldn't have dared. Pippa half expected them to salute.

He ushered them into the studio and introduced them around. And that was how they met Ritchie who, for pure entertainment value, was one of the great experiences of Pippa's life.

It seemed that nobody had told Ritchie that this was a small cable station. His hair was elegantly blow-dried, his puce shirt was open to the waist, showing an expanse of tanned chest against which a gold chain gleamed. When he spoke, his voice resonated. He gave instructions as though beaming messages to the four corners of the world.

One person hung on his every word, and that was Derek, a young man of downtrodden appearance who rejoiced in the title of assistant and ferried Ritchie's inhaler from place to place, to help him cope with the kind of crises that engulfed all great men.

Ritchie greeted Luke with the respect due to a star who had single-handedly doubled the channel's subscribers. But his version of respect was like nobody else's.

"Luke, baby, *glad* you could make it!" he exclaimed, as though Luke had risen from a sick bed.

"I always make it, Ritch," Luke observed mildly.

Ritchie made a sound like a ruptured hyena. "You have to have your little joke, Luke baby! Now, are things all right? Is everything here just as you like it?"

"Everything's just as it always is."

"That's what I like to hear. A satisfied customer. I just know today's shows are going to be the most wonderful ever—"

"I've a couple of people I'd like you to meet," Luke said, breaking into the cloud of hyperbole. "This is Pippa, and this is Josie, her daughter—and mine."

Ritchie was wide-eyed. *"You…have…a…daughter?"* he gasped, in a tone that implied Luke had invented nuclear physics. He surveyed Pippa and Josie as though they were an alien species. "Well now—well now—I just never dreamed—"

"No reason why you should," Luke said affably. "But they're spending some time with me, and I'd like them to enjoy themselves here."

"I'll make that my personal responsibility," Ritchie declared with fervor.

"Seats in the front row."

"Well, that might be a little difficult—"

"Seats in the front row, Ritch."

"Whatever you say. Derek, where are you? My inhaler."

At last the studio settled down and the rehearsal began. It fascinated Pippa that Luke got through this as fast as possible, passing from dish to dish with the barest outline of what he intended to say.

"Don't you have some sort of script?" she asked when he'd finished.

He shuddered. "Perish the thought. I just say what comes into my head. It's usually okay."

"And if it isn't, they can always do a retake," Josie said, beaming.

Luke regarded her with fatherly disfavor. "Yes,"

he said through gritted teeth. "They can always do a retake."

"I should have warned you," Pippa said, chuckling, "one of the joys of kids is that they're always puncturing your little balloon."

He grinned. "I'll be lucky if I still *have* a balloon when my daughter's finished. Okay, here are your seats, middle of the front row. I have to go now. Bye! Have fun."

He stooped and kissed Josie's cheek, laid a hand on Pippa's shoulder and kissed her lightly on the mouth. Then he was gone, leaving her to realize that Luke had kissed her for the first time in eleven years.

It had been over before she'd had time to think, the kind of casual salute he probably gave to women every day, thinking nothing of it. But it lingered on her mouth like honey.

Be sensible, she thought. It meant nothing to him, and you're not an adolescent anymore. But she felt as though a drop of water had fallen onto her parched lips after years in the desert. Her defenses tottered alarmingly. She didn't want to be sensible. She wanted Luke to kiss her again. She wanted to kiss him back and tell him how lonely she'd been without him.

She brought herself back to reality with an effort. The audience was beginning to stream in, and soon the seats were full of laughing, chattering people. Ritchie came out and gave a brief warm-up talk, then the lights went down on the studio, up on the set, and there was Luke, wearing his most infectious grin, greeting the crowd as if they were old friends.

He wore a red apron and red chef's hat and he

had a feast of cherry dishes. For the next hour he held them spellbound. Pippa watched in admiration as Luke produced a great, barnstorming performance. He had the gift of being able to project his real self. There was the cheeky charm, the crazy clowning, the hint that he'd found the secret of making life fun. And behind it, the perfect organization, each detail under control, everything planned just as he wanted it. In fact, there was Luke, writ large.

Pippa and Josie joined in the laughter with everyone else. Josie's eyes were shining and she applauded loud and long. "Isn't Daddy wonderful?" she whispered to Pippa.

"Yes, darling. He's wonderful."

After the first show there was a break for lunch, and Josie and Pippa picnicked with Luke in his dressing room. Josie chattered a mile a minute, while Luke grinned. But the grin was wiped off his face when his phone rang.

"Okay, okay," he said, sounding exasperated. "We'll just have to find something else." As he hung up he was audibly grinding his teeth. "My suppliers have let me down. Now a couple of tomorrow's dishes have to be changed."

"Can you do it at such short notice?" Josie asked anxiously. "I mean, can you do the rest of today's show and think up new recipes?"

He grinned and tweaked her nose. "For genius, nothing is impossible."

"Yes, Daddy, but can *you* do it?" Josie asked, straight-faced.

Luke flung up his hands. "Great!" he told Pippa. "You've been teaching my kid to be a smart aleck.

Come on, brat. Back to work, and your old man will try not to disappoint you.''

Josie giggled, and they went out with their arms about each other's waists.

It all started again. Ritchie came out again, reminding the audience to greet Luke with the same enthusiasm as before, but he needn't have bothered. They adored him, and the cheer, when he appeared again, raised the roof. He'd changed into fresh jeans and sweater, and the red hat and apron had been replaced by green and white, suggesting the salads he was about to create.

Josie was caught up in the general excitement, but Pippa found herself standing back and seeing Luke as he appeared to the rest of the world. It was a curious experience, like looking at him down a long tunnel, and she had the strange feeling that she knew him better. He was a man who could give a little of himself to a million people, but not all of himself to anyone. She should have known that long ago.

He seemed to have inexhaustible energy, because after a brief pause he was off again on the third show, and it was as fresh and spontaneous as the first. Then it was over, and the crowd was streaming out, leaving Josie and Pippa alone in their seats. Now that everyone could relax, Josie took the chance to explore the studio. Ritchie flopped down beside Pippa like a rag doll.

''Every time I swear I can't go through it again,'' he moaned. ''But somehow I find the nervous energy. The question is, how much longer?''

''As long as the ratings are good, I suppose,'' Pippa said, amused.

''You're right. Only the public really counts,

doesn't it? That great hydra-headed crowd out there, baying for its pound of flesh.''

"We'll just have to hope that *Luke* can keep producing the goods," she said demurely.

"Of course," he replied with an edge on his voice. "Nobody knows what he owes to Luke more than I do."

"I'll bet you do."

He gave her a sour look and went in search of a more appreciative audience.

In the car, on the way home, she related this conversation, and Luke shouted with laughter. "That's my Pippa," he said appreciatively. "Never stood any nonsense from anyone. And he certainly offers himself as a target."

"What about your problem?" Pippa asked. "Did it sort itself out?"

"No, it got a lot worse, and I'm afraid I'm not going to be good company this evening. I've got to spend tonight working out new recipes and cooking them myself, as well."

"So we'll help you," Pippa said. "I can cook you know."

"No, really? I had no idea."

"If you weren't driving this car I'd kick your shins. I'll do the supper. You get on with being the genius of the screen. And don't you dare hover over me, sticking your nose in. You won't be driving a car then."

"Yes, *ma'am!*"

He tried to be virtuous. He and Josie seated themselves at his computer, and before her fascinated eyes he called up recipe after recipe, considering, rejecting, analyzing, amending. But his mind was only half on the job. He couldn't resist looking over his shoulder at Pippa, moving about the kitchen—*his* kitchen—opening *his* doors and drawers.

"Dad," Josie muttered, reading his tension. "I wouldn't if I was you."

"I was only going to—"

"Well, don't! Not unless you want to be bopped on the head."

"Look," he said, also muttering, "I just want to show her where things are. She won't understand my plan."

"Yes, she will. She's got the same one."

"What do you mean?"

"Mom's organized the kitchen at home just like this. It's smaller, but the plan's the same. Knives here, chopping board there, blender in the cupboard on the right, scales in the cupboard on the left. Same as you. She says it's how you reorganized Ma's kitchen years ago."

"Really?" He was fascinated.

"And she goes mad if anything's out of place. Honestly, you'd think the world was going to end if anything's just a little untidy."

"Pippa? Tidy? You're kidding me."

"Why?"

"I knew her before you, remember?"

"Was she untidy then?"

"Was she unti— Let me tell you...."

He stopped, realizing that his memories of discarded clothes littering their room were hardly suitable for a child's ears. "Never mind," he said hastily. "Look, she's driving me nuts."

"Dad, leave it."

"Yes, dear." He subsided.

But it was more than flesh and blood could stand. Within minutes he jumped up. "Pippa, not that saucepan—"

She whirled, eyes flashing, ladle in hand. "Josie, get him out of here—*now!*"

"Let's go," Josie said briskly. "We've got work to do. You need a whole pile of new ingredients, and we'd better go out and buy them from an all-night supermarket."

"Don't think there is one around here," Luke said stubbornly.

"Dad," Josie said patiently, "I watch American movies. I know there's always an all-night supermarket. Now come on. I'm not ready to be an orphan yet."

"What's this orphan talk?"

"You seen the way Mom's wielding that ladle?"

Businesslike, she scooped up the list he'd been jotting, scooped up his jacket, scooped up his wallet. Finally, almost as an afterthought, she scooped up her father and shepherded him out of the door. Pippa heard their voices fading.

"You should never take Mom on when she has that light in her eye...."

"I believe you, I believe you...."

They were back in less than an hour, laden with bags. Pippa had prepared a meal that could be eaten "on the run" because she knew that once Luke's creative flame started burning he had attention for nothing else. His charm would vanish, replaced by, "Yes," "No," "Hurry up," and "You're in my way!" because a man bent on the culinary equivalent of the Sistine Chapel had no time for social niceties.

She was all set to explain this to Josie, lest she be upset, but there was no need. The youngster transformed herself into Luke's lieutenant, rushing to do his bidding quickly and quietly. She never forgot where anything was, and sometimes seemed to understand what he wanted before he spoke. When not needed she effaced herself without making a production of it. She was like another professional, so intent on making the finished product perfect that nothing else mattered. In fact, she was her father's daughter.

"Josie, where—?"

"Here," she said, putting it into his hand.

"I need another dip—no, two. One spicy—tomato, radish, cayenne. One bland—yogurt, cucumber, crushed garlic, lemon juice." He was talking to himself now.

"Tomatoes," Josie muttered, diving for them. "Cayenne, yogurt, cucumber, garlic, lemon juice...."

In seconds she had everything lined up ready to go. Luke inspected, gave her brief instructions and returned to the oven. Pippa made notes, but she hardly felt needed. The other two were in a world of their own, which gave her a fleeting moment's sadness, but she suppressed it. This was just what she'd hoped for.

At last they were finished. Luke gave Josie an appreciative grin. "I wish I had a few like you working for me, especially on the show." Suddenly he whirled on Pippa. *"Hey!"*

"Luke, no."

He seized her shoulders. "But it's a fantastic idea. I need someone who knows what I'm doing here, and there isn't time to rehearse anyone else. Josie knows it all. She helped create this masterpiece.''

''But how will you introduce her?''

''As my daughter, what else? You'd like to do it, wouldn't you, honey?''

''Oh, yes!'' Josie was jumping up and down.

''But only if Mommy says so,'' Luke added quickly.

''Mommy, please, *please!* Daddy, make her say yes.''

''Honey, I can't go against your mother. If she won't let you—''

''Luke Danton, you are the most devious, conniving, unscrupulous, unprincipled—''

His smile took her breath away. ''I guess that means yes.''

''Yes, Mommy, *yes!*''

''Oh, all right, yes.''

Father and daughter promptly went into a mad, leaping dance about the kitchen. Pippa watched them, smiling, and was caught off guard when he suddenly shot an arm around her waist and swept her into the dance, whirling her around and around until she was giddy.

''Whoa!'' he said at last. ''Hey, are you all right?''

''Yes, fine,'' she gasped.

''You don't look so good,'' he said, looking into her face, concerned.

''My head's spinning. You went too fast for me. I need to sit down.''

''Okay, but not on one of those high stools. Let's go next door and you can sit down properly.''

''Mommy?'' Josie said, frowning a little.

"I'm fine, darling. Your father's a madman, but that's okay."

Luke still had his arm around her waist, and her hands were clasped behind his neck, steadying herself. It was natural for him to lift her up, announce, "Taxi service, ma'am!" and proceed into the big room, still carrying her.

"Clown," she said fondly.

He set her down on the sofa. "Are you really all right, Pippa? You looked a bit strange back there."

"Well, I'm just not used to being spun around like a top by a man who seems to think we're still a couple of kids."

He grinned. "Well, you always did say I'd never grow up. So did my mom, and she ought to know. Come to think of it, every woman I've ever known has said it. Can't think why."

"Neither can I," she said tenderly, brushing back a tousled lock from his forehead. "But it's only a matter of time before Josie starts saying it."

"True. You always did understand me better than anyone, Pippa."

"Now you stop that!"

"Stop what?"

"You know what I mean. The little-boy charm. And the wide-eyed innocence that you're doing now. I know all your tricks. You honed them on me, remember?"

"Only some of them," he said wickedly. "I've learned a few more since then."

"Well, keep them to yourself. I'm a respectable middle-aged woman."

"Middle-aged, my foot! You're not thirty yet."

"Yes, I am," she said with dignity. "I was thirty last birthday."

"Liar. You'll be thirty next birthday."

He had remembered her age that precisely. She had to struggle not to smile with the pleasure.

"You are not middle-aged," he said firmly. "And you were *never* respectable."

"I was before I met you."

He raised an eyebrow. "Well, there's no going back to *that*," he said wickedly, and kissed the end of her nose.

Then he seemed to hesitate, his face close to hers, his eyes smiling. Her heartbeat became dangerously uneven as she realized that in a moment he would kiss her, perhaps lightly as he'd done in the studio, perhaps more deeply. And she wanted that so much. She didn't care about being sensible anymore. All the long, lonely years without him were an ache that could only be eased by being in his arms. His mouth was just the same—mobile, seductive, promising so much that his body would fulfil. Just one kiss. Just one—

"Mom— Dad—"

Luke stood up swiftly. At any other time Pippa would have been amused by the self-conscious smile he assumed. Now she could hardly contain her disappointment. When Luke returned to the kitchen, she stayed where she was, trying to believe it was for the best.

What about all your good resolutions? You swore this wouldn't happen. Pull yourself together. You're a mother of a ten-year-old daughter, you're not a teenager. You're old enough to know better.

After a while she got shakily to her feet and made

her way back to the kitchen, where Luke was reading the details of the new creation into his computer,
and Josie was sampling the product.

It was late before they finished cooking three different stages of three dishes, but everyone was up
early the next day, too excited to sleep. Luke packed
everything up with reverent hands and drove slowly
to the studio. His two employees were there before
him. He was on hot coals as he relinquished his
treasures into their hands, and it was only Josie's
promise that, "I'll keep an eye on them, Daddy,"
that reconciled him to the parting.

"And me," Pippa said, amused. "I'll look after
them, too. Of course, I know I'm not up to Josie's
standard, but—"

"Sorry. Yes, please go with them, explain what's
what. I'll go and have a word with Ritchie."

As Pippa joined the little party marching in sol-
emn procession to the kitchen, Ritchie bore down
on Luke, all flags flying. "I just *know* these are going to be the best shows ever," he declared. "Sure
you had some problems with new dishes, but I just
know you're going to tell me it's all sorted out."

"You mean you're scared I'm not," Luke said,
reading this accurately. "No sweat, Ritchie. I invented two completely new recipes, with Josie's
help."

"Why, isn't that sweet!" Ritchie seemed almost
overwhelmed.

"I knew you'd love it. You're going to love the
next bit even more. Josie comes on the show with
me—star billing for the day. The next generation."

"The next—" Ritchie blanched. "You mean you're going to tell people she's your kid?"

"Sure I'm going to tell them. What's the point of having a kid if nobody knows?"

"Well, pardon me, but nobody has known for the past few years. I don't recall your rushing to tell the world that you had a growing daughter."

"Well, I'm telling the world now. It's a wonderful idea."

"I don't think so. I really don't think so."

"She's going to wear an apron and chef's hat that match mine, and she'll look great in them."

Ritchie took a deep breath and rallied his forces. His smile was ghastly. "Luke, baby, the chicks like to think you're available, know what I mean? Okay, we're all unmarried fathers these days—"

"You, Ritch? Surely not?"

Ritchie gulped. "You'd be surprised at some of the guys I could tell you about. But," he added, rushing on before Luke could make an issue of it, "we don't have to parade it. You've got a reputation as a stud, and you've got to play up to it. When they eat your dishes, the guys tell themselves they can have a wild sex life like Luke Danton, and the chicks feel they've got Luke Danton in bed with them. I've seen some of those hot e-mails you get. And then you come out with a kid? It spoils your image. Get real. Get *rid!*"

For the first time it occurred to Luke that he actively disliked Ritchie. In a colder voice than the producer had ever heard him use before he said, "It's lucky for you that Josie's out of earshot, because if she'd heard that, you'd be in big trouble.

She is my daughter, and she is coming on the show with me. Got it?''

"Got it, got it!" Ritchie said.

"Plus I want to change the running order. This show goes out first."

"But that's the day after tomorrow."

"Right. That way she'll get to see it before she leaves."

Hope gleamed in the producer's eye. "She's leaving?"

"Just do it, Ritch. And get it perfect."

"Yes, yes, whatever you say. Get it perfect, put it on first. Tell all the world. Watch the ratings slump. Cut your throat. Oh, God, I wish I was dead! *Derek, my inhaler!*''

...thinking about a phone call I've got to make. My folks always watch the show, and if Josie's going to appear the day after tomorrow—" He floundered into silence, the picture of guilt.

A monstrous suspicion grew in Pippa. "Luke, does your family know you have a daughter?"

He shook his head. "Don't get mad at me. If I'd told Mom everything years ago, she'd have come down on me like a duck on a June bug."

"That's nothing to what she's going to do now."

"I know, I know. Look, I wish I'd done it but—"

"But you did what was easiest, as always."

"Lord, but you sound like her!"

"I'm a mother, too. It comes with the territory."

"Okay, so I've got to pick up the phone and explain before she sees the show."

"Phone, nothing. You get over there and tell her to her face."

and the looks of healthy animals that lived as they pleased.

She reckoned it would take Luke at least a couple of hours, but after only half an hour she saw his Porsche returning. Obviously nobody had been at home, she thought, and he'd come straight back. But then another car followed his into the drive, and an endless river of people streamed out. Aghast, Pippa realized that Luke had brought the family with him, and not willingly, either, if his helpless shrug up to her on the balcony was anything to go by.

The next moment they were all pouring through the back door, and Pippa was emerging nervously to meet them. Luke's plump little mother surveyed her fiercely. "Are you Pippa?" she demanded.

"I...yes—" The rest was lost in a suffocating embrace. Pippa was half a head taller, but somehow Luke's mother still managed to engulf her.

Then her husband, so tall that it was clear where Luke's height came from, and with a face made for laughter. He, too, hugged her, with a great roar of delight. Zak was the same as in his picture, a younger version of Luke, not quite so tall, a little heavier, but with the same smile and the same air of knowing the world was his for the taking. Becky had gray eyes full of humor, and a no-nonsense manner than Pippa took to at once.

They were allowed only a moment before his mother shunted them aside and hugged Pippa again, saying, "We should have met long ago, but better late than never."

"Yes," Pippa agreed, liking her instinctively.

Luke made the mistake of putting himself forward. "Mom, why don't we—"

She rounded on him. "Did anyone speak to you?"

"No, Mom."

"You speak when you're spoken to, and be grateful you're being spoken to at all."

"Yes, Mom."

Becky and Zak exchanged grins. Luke glared at them, but otherwise subsided meekly. Suddenly a silence fell. All heads turned to the kitchen door where Josie stood rubbing the sleep out of her eyes. Pippa was about to introduce her, but some instinct held her silent. She knew it had been a wise instinct, when Luke slipped his arm around his daughter's shoulders and said simply, "This is Josie. She's mine." He looked down at his daughter. "This is my family—your family now."

Everyone was waiting for his mother's reaction, and it came quickly. The short woman and the tall child were almost at eye level. They surveyed each other. Then Josie gave her slow, gorgeous smile, and Luke's mom gasped.

"Clarrie!" she cried. And burst into tears.

"Who's Clarrie?" Pippa asked under cover of the commotion.

"She was Mom's kid sister," Becky told her. "She died years ago. I've only seen pictures, but I guess there is a resemblance."

She, too, was swept up in the introductions, then Zak, then his mom again, then dad. Pippa feared that Josie might find this overwhelming, but not for long. As she'd already proved in the television studio, the child had inherited her father's natural self-possession when "on show." Josie sorted her thoughts out fast, said, "I'd better get dressed," and vanished.

Pippa followed her and took out some clean jeans and a T-shirt. "Are you all right, darling?"

"Mom," Josie said, awed, "I've got grandparents."

"Yes, you never had them before."

"Isn't it great?"

"Yes, darling, it's great."

Luke was waiting as they emerged from the bedroom. "I'm sorry about this," he muttered. "I barely got the words out when they pounced on me and dragged me out to the car. I didn't even get the chance to call you first."

"It's all right. I'm glad they've taken to her so well. And at least you're still in one piece."

"I am now. But boy, the earful I got from Mom!"

"And your father?"

"No, he lets her do it for him."

"It's nice that they're so pleased."

"Are you kidding? This is their first grandchild. They're over the moon. Zak and Becky are pretty thrilled, too, because it takes the pressure off them to settle down and start breeding."

Zak, who'd come out into the hall, grinned. "Trust my big brother to come to the rescue," he said. "Pippa, she's a great kid. We're all going to love her. And you."

He followed this up with a hug. Pippa was glad the hall lighting was low so that they shouldn't see the sudden tears in her eyes. All these years she'd thought she knew what she was missing, but there was so much more that she'd never dreamed of. She surreptitiously wiped her eyes and went back to the kitchen with the other two.

It seemed that Luke's dad would monopolize his new granddaughter. They were seated side by side at the bar, drinking milk shakes and talking nineteen to the dozen. Now and then one of the others would join in, only to be edged out by his dad. Luke's mother surveyed them with great satisfaction.

"He's found someone his own age at last," she confided to Josie.

Pippa soon saw that she was right. Between the man of sixty and the girl of ten there was a true meeting of minds. Pippa watched in fascination, beginning to understand Luke as never before.

At that moment his dad's voice rose in horror. "You mean you've never been to Disneyland?"

Wide-eyed, Josie shook her head. "Never," she said mournfully.

"Josie," Pippa said, scandalized, "you stop playing Orphan Annie right now."

"Don't spoil it for him," his wife said quickly.
"He loves the place. Now he's got a cast-iron excuse. You wouldn't want to deprive him of it, would
you?"

"I guess not," Pippa said, dazed.

In no time Disneyland became the agenda for next
day. Zak and Becky had to work, but the other five
would drive over to Anaheim. With that point settled
the family departed, leaving Luke's house alarmingly quiet.

Next day she, Luke and Josie drove over to his
parents' house. His mom greeted Pippa and Josie as
if they'd parted a year ago instead of a few hours,
and she took Pippa aside. "I wanted to show you
this," she said, holding out a photograph. "It was
Clarrie."

The picture was forty years old and taken by a
very basic camera. Even so, Pippa was amazed at
the likeness. She was used to thinking of Josie as
resembling herself, but now she saw that the child's
heart-shaped face was the same as the one in the
picture. So, too, was the slight upward tilt of her
nose.

"It broke my heart when I lost her," Luke's mom
confided. "Well, I guess I've kind of got her back
now."

Pippa was shaken. She'd half suspected that the
resemblance to Clarrie was an illusion, invented by
Luke's mother. The discovery that it was real
seemed to change everything in some subtle way.
Josie really did belong in this family. She even
looked different to Pippa's eyes.

"I'm glad," she said.

The older woman eyed her. "You look like a nice

girl. How come you didn't want to marry my Luke?''

"I—what's he been saying?''

"He says he asked you to marry him and you said no. Isn't that true?''

Pippa's jaw dropped. "Well, he's got a nerve ,'' she said wrathfully. "He—I—well, yes, technically I suppose it's true, in a sort of way. But I could hear it in his voice that he was only asking out of duty—''

"Duty? *Luke?*'' echoed Luke's mother.

"Well, there certainly wasn't any other reason. You should have heard how relieved he was when I refused!''

His mother's eyes were kind and shrewd. "So, no meant yes, right?''

"Right! At least, it would have been if he'd really wanted me, but we sort of had a deal—no strings, and so I, well, you know—''

"Sure I know. He's my son. And his father's son, heaven help us all!''

Pippa was breathing hard. "So he played the injured innocent, did he?''

"And good!''

"I can just hear him. 'Mom, I wanted to marry her, but she brushed me off.' I'm going to make him sorry he was born.''

"Hey, that's a mother's privilege. You wait in line.''

"No, *you* wait in line,'' Pippa said firmly. "The first bite belongs to me.''

His mother chuckled. "Be my guest.''

"Maisie, are you coming?'' Dad called.

"You hush up!" she told him. "I'm talking to my daughter-in-law."

"Mrs. Danton—" Pippa said hurriedly.

"Mom!"

"Mom, I'm not—"

"You are as far as I'm concerned," she declared, adding, with a belligerent eye on her son on the far side of the room, "and if some people had any sense, you would be."

It was wonderful to be so accepted, but Pippa had seen the sudden alert look that came into Josie's face, and she took the first chance to mutter in Luke's ear, "Please don't let her talk like that. It might give Josie the wrong idea."

"I can't help the way Mom talks."

"You've got to. I don't want Josie thinking we might get married. Please, Luke, this is very important."

"All right," he said, giving her a strange look.

They made the trip to Anaheim in his father's car, with his mother sitting up front with him and the other three in the back. His dad was describing Disneyland to Josie, who was listening wide-eyed. Pippa sat quietly, trying to talk herself into a reasonable frame of mind, but it was hard after what she'd just heard.

Oh, if she could only get Luke to herself for just five minutes! She would kick his shins, stamp on his toes, wring his neck and boil him in oil. And then she'd do something *really* painful. If she could only think of it. By the time they arrived, her temper had worked up a fine head of steam.

Josie was speechless with the wonder of her first

sight of Disneyland. Her grandparents took charge of her, happy as kids themselves.

"Let me show you the shops," Luke said, taking Pippa's hand. To the others he called, "You go on. Don't wait for us."

"Should we do that?" Pippa asked.

"You think it takes more than two people to look after our daughter? Anyway, she's busy wrapping them both around her little finger. We'd only cramp her style."

"You're right," she said. "This is a good chance for a private talk."

"Why do I feel suddenly nervous?"

"Because you have every reason to."

"Pippa, do you know that your eyes are glittering? In the old days they only did that when you were good 'n' mad about something. Usually me."

"Well, ten out of ten for observation! How dare you tell your mother that you asked me to marry you!"

"But I did."

"In a pig's eye you did!"

"I asked you, and you said no," he protested.

"Luke, there are ways and ways of asking people. There's when you're desperate for them to say yes, and when you're desperate for them to say no. No prizes for guessing which one you chose."

"And you think you're a mind reader, huh?"

"I didn't have to read your mind. You told it to me right from the start. No marriage, no domesticity, no babies, no being tied down. You couldn't have been plainer. So I took the hint. When you raised the subject of marriage—at a safe distance of five thousand miles—I said what you wanted me to say, just as I always did.''

"Well, I'll be—"

"And then you went and told your mother it was all my fault—"

"Pippa, she asked me why I didn't marry you, and I said that I asked you and you said no—which was true—"

"It was a half-truth at best."

"Okay, I'll talk to her, tell how exactly how it was."

"No, need. I already have."

"So that's what you were doing with your heads together, pulling me apart—"

"I'd *like* to pull you apart," she seethed.

"Gee, this is like the old days! You wouldn't listen to reason then, and you won't now."

"Reason? Hah! *You* talking reason? That I should like to hear!"

"Pippa, you wouldn't recognize reason if it hit you in the eye."

"You know the answer to that."

"If you aren't the most ornery woman—I'll swear I—oh, to hell with it!"

"Hey, what do you think you're doing?" Luke had grabbed her hand and was hauling her after him.

"This way," he called over his shoulder.

"*Luke—*"

"Hurry." The next moment he was climbing aboard a horse-drawn carriage, giving her no choice but to follow. His hands were warm and firm, pulling her aboard, then just holding her while he laughed into her eyes.

"No," she said, trying to be firm. "I will not let you shut me up like this. Do you understand?"

"There's Mom and Dad with Josie. Wave to them."

Josie was carrying a huge candy floss. She waved ecstatically, and Pippa could do nothing but wave back, smiling to cover the fact that she was fuming. "I'll get you for this," she muttered.

"Look happy, or she won't be happy."

"Considering I'd like to chuck you in the nearest fountain I'm looking amazingly happy," Pippa said through gritted teeth. "And just what do you think you're doing?"

"I'm sliding my hand around your shoulder, friendly fashion—even if you don't deserve it," he said through his smile.

"I feel as friendly as a python at the moment," she said through hers. "Remove your hand right now."

"Nah, they'd suspect something. It's more convincing if I just tighten it around your shoulder—"

"I'm warning you—"

"And then draw you closer to me—like this—"

"You let me go this instant—*Luke!*"

He mustn't kiss her, because if he did her heart would melt, and she would forget why she was mad at him. She wanted to stay mad. That was always safest with Luke.

But it was too late to tell him he mustn't, and he wasn't taking any notice, anyway. Out of the corner of her eye she could see his mom, dad and Josie, all laughing with delight. Then the carriage passed on and they were out of sight.

"They've gone now, you can let me go," she said.

"Nope."

"You can't kiss me in the middle of Disney-land."

"What does it feel like I'm doing?"

She gave up arguing. The feeling that was spreading through her was taking over, silencing thought. It wasn't desire, or any physical sensation. It was sheer happiness, of a kind she'd almost forgotten: the happiness of being with this one man, in his arms, with nothing else to worry about—at least for a brief time.

And she had almost wasted that time in squabbling. Was she mad?

She kissed him back, then settled blissfully in the crook of his arm, feeling the years and the worries and the weariness fall away. Surely she could allow herself this one day?

"You're a scoundrel," she said. "But I forgive you."

"You always did. Not mad at me anymore?"

"I expect I am, really—only I forget why."

"It doesn't matter. Let's have fun."

"Oh, yes, please."

When the carriage halted he gave her his hand, helping her down as gallantly as any squire with his lady, and steered her straight into a shop where a collection of cooks were making chocolates before an admiring crowd. Luke bought a bagful and they strolled out again, munching.

"When I was a kid I used to bring girls here," he mused. "We all did. There was a set routine. You started with Sleeping Beauty's Castle to put her in a romantic mood, then you progressed to Thunder Mountain because when the cars went up and down she'd let you hold her tight. The clincher was the Haunted Mansion, because with any luck she'd hold *you* tight!''

She chuckled. ''You're evil!''

''I know. It's been very useful.''

They laughed together, and she slipped her arm about his waist.

''Shall we start from the beginning?'' he asked, ''and see if my technique's improved over the years?''

''No need. Let's take the early stages as read, and just wander.''

''That sounds good.''

As they strolled along Main Street he said, ''I suppose in a sense we really have just met.'' There was a question in his eyes.

''Yes,'' she said, understanding him.

It was the perfect way. To meet again, without memories or pain, nothing in fact but the charm they had always had for each other: to meet practically as children, in an enchanted world.

Since coming to Los Angeles, Pippa had had a sense of unreality, as though she'd strayed into a hologram, and if she turned the wrong knob everything would vanish. Now that sense was heightened. She'd been given the chance to find Luke again in a dream, and when that dream was over the wounds would have healed, leaving her strong enough to face whatever she had to.

They stopped in a gift shop and he gallantly presented her with a Mickey Mouse necklace and a pair of earrings to match, assuring her solemnly that this had always "paid great dividends." Whereupon she made a sound that he called a snigger. She denied it, he insisted, and they were still arguing as they climbed aboard the railway.

When they left it they were arguing about something else in a manner that might kindly be described as "Yah! Sucks! Boo!" Josie chanced to come across them, and declared, enchanted, that she'd heard her father say, "So there!" although he insisted he'd actually said, "Take care," as Pippa neared a step. Pippa was unable to settle the argument as she was laughing too much to have heard what he said.

The two parties had lunch together. Josie, sporting a necklace and earring set that exactly matched Pippa's, talked nonstop. She was totally happy, not only with Disneyland, but with her new family, and Pippa's heart eased.

Afterward they split up again, Josie and entourage heading for Thunder Mountain, and Luke and Pippa for the calmer delights of the steamboat.

As they leaned on the rail watching the water drift past, Luke said suddenly, "Pippa, can I ask you something?"

"Sure."

"If you could go back and wave a magic wand over the past few years—what would you change?"

Dangerous territory. The sun was so warm and the air so sweet that for a moment she almost admitted, "I would have liked to spend them with you." But to say that was to put emotional pressure on him, and risk everything she'd gained. Safer to pass it off lightly.

"I might not have wanted to run a guest house," she mused. "They're all lovely people, but it's the culinary equivalent of being exiled to Siberia. I created a new recipe once, a fruit dish with cherries and lemon and a mystery ingredient. I was feeling cross about being 'exiled' with all the stodge I had to cook, so I called it Siberian cherries. Josie loved it but everyone else thought I was mad."

"I wouldn't have," he said seriously.

"No, you'd have understood. I could always talk to you about things that meant a lot to me, and you picked it up at once. Other people just looked blank."

"It was like that for me," he said, much struck. "We talked the same kind of nonsense and understood the same kind of world, and we were almost telepathic. Do you remember how we used to finish off each other's sentences?"

"That's right." It was coming back to her. "I hated it if anyone else tried to do that, but I didn't mind with you, because you always got it right."

"So did you. Always." He straightened up, alert as though a momentous thought had come to him. "That's what we really had, wasn't it? The rest was...icing on the cake."

"Beautiful icing," she reminded him with a smile.

"The best. But underneath, we had a perfect cake, too." He took her hand and looked at it. "Wouldn't you change anything else?"

"No," she said after a moment.

"Nothing? Nothing at all?"

"What happened gave me Josie. And she's perfect. Thank you, Luke. Thank you for Josie. Thank you for everything. I've wanted to say that for a long time."

He was still tracing patterns on the back of her hand. "Nobody ever got to me the way you did."

"Nor me. We were very young and very intense about everything, weren't we? Too intense, maybe."

"I don't think so."

Something in his voice caught her, made her look up quickly, but he was still studying her hand, as though he feared to meet her eyes.

"Luke, I—"

There was a slight thump as the boat reached the landing stage. All around them people were getting to their feet, preparing to disembark. He raised her hand and kissed it and led her from the boat.

He kept hold of her hand until they met up again with the others, then let it discreetly fall. A riotous meal was followed by the fireworks display. Josie was openmouthed, staring up into the dark sky as it was flooded with brilliance. Luke's parents, too, seemed to be seeing it all for the first time.

Nobody was looking at Luke and Pippa. In the midst of that huge crowd they were invisible. Luke's hands were on either side of her face, his thumbs gently caressing her cheeks. His eyes were warm, and then his lips were on hers, as tenderly as a boy with his first kiss.

"Pippa," he whispered. "Pippa, my Pippa—"

He kissed her mouth softly, almost reverently. Her returning kiss was the same, loving rather than passionate. It was all part of the dream, and as a dream she would take it, not asking more, for that was when dreams died.

He seemed to understand that, too, for he drew back and rested his arms on her shoulders, his forehead against hers, his smiling eyes close to hers. Suddenly a tremor overtook him. In a shaking voice he said, *"Oh, Pippa!"* and pulled her close, not kissing her but burying his face against her neck in a bear hug. *"Pippa, Pippa, Pippa!"*

She hugged him back in the same way, her eyes closed as she guessed his were, so that the world contained nothing but their shared warmth and the tightness of their arms about each other. And neither of them saw the three interested pairs of eyes watching them.

It was midnight when they reached the home of Luke's parents, but they stayed for a quick snack. Pippa would have been glad to fade into the background and let Josie be the star, but Luke's mom had other ideas. She had called Pippa "my daughter-in-law," and it clearly hadn't been an idle remark. Now she treated her with conspicuous honor, and although she only repeated the dangerous words once, her feelings permeated the air. Pippa felt awkward, but Luke seemed surprisingly unfazed when she tackled him about it.

"She's a mother," he said. "It goes with the territory. She's been trying to settle me down with a good woman for years."

"Someone should tell her that good women give

you a wide berth," Pippa replied crisply. "This is about Josie, not me."

"Well, she's not happy about the fact that her new granddaughter is going away in a few days," he retorted. "Maybe she's trying to tell you something."

"No, it's you she's trying to tell, and you ought to warn her off, Luke. It's not fair to anyone."

His mother called him at that point, so he didn't have to reply, but he gave her a strange look.

At last it was time to say goodbye, but only until the next night when the family was coming over to Luke's home to watch the show. His mother hugged Pippa fiercely. As they were in the front hall she seemed to remember something.

"Luke, before you go—"

"Yes, Mom?"

"Come here."

Obediently he went to stand in front of his mother, looking down at her, smiling. The next moment he was reeling back from the sharpest box on the ears she had ever given him.

"Hey, Mom!"

"That's for not telling us! Ten years of our grandchild we've missed. You should be ashamed."

"I am, Mom. Promise." He backed hastily from the martial light in his mother's eye.

He got hastily into the car, rubbing his ear. As they pulled away from the curb he complained to Pippa, "If I'm not being bullied by her, I'm being bullied by you. If I'm not being bullied by you, I'm being bullied by Claudia. If I'm not being bullied by Claudia, I'm being bullied by my daughter. That guy who talked about the monstrous regiment of women sure knew what he was talking about.'' There was a giggle from the back seat. ''And you can hush up!''

Josie made no answer, but after a few minutes Luke became aware of a strange sound coming from the back seat.

''Josie? You're not crying, are you?''

''Not really, it's just—we came all this way, and we don't have much time together, and…and you had to get mad at me…and—'' She choked into silence.

Luke slammed the car into the side of the road. He was out in a moment, pulling open the rear door, flinging himself inside, taking his daughter in his arms.

''Honey, I'm sorry, I'm not really mad at you. Please…please darling, don't cry. There baby… please…I can't stand it…just tell me what you want, Daddy will make it right.''

''Luke,'' Pippa said patiently, ''it's like taking candy from a baby. Mind you, I fell for it the first few times, too.''

''She's upset—'' Another suspicious sound made him look sharply at Josie. The tears had magically vanished, and the child was making unconvincing efforts to control her laughter. ''Why you…!''

''Oh, Daddy, if you could see your face!''

''You…?''

''I learned how to do it in drama class at school.''

''You little wretch—*come here!*'' He swept her up into a hug so fierce that she gasped. She returned it plus interest, her arms tight about his neck until he almost choked. Pippa rested her arm on the back of her seat and her chin on her arm, watching them with deep satisfaction.

She had all she'd asked for when she came here, including a return of the dream, for just one day. And now that the day was over, she had no complaints. She was far richer than she had been this morning.

Chapter Eight

By the time they reached home, Josie was fast asleep on the back seat. Luke carried her inside and laid her gently on the bed. Josie awoke just enough for Pippa to help her undress, then nodded off again at once. They crept out.

Pippa yawned. "I'll just have some tea, and then I'll turn in, too."

"Not yet," Luke begged, sliding his arms around her and trying to kiss her.

"Luke, no," she said, pressing a hand against his chest.

"What is it?"

"Today was lovely, but we were on vacation—"

"Well, we still are." He tightened his arms and this time managed to touch her mouth with his own. She was shaken by the temptation to yield. It had

been a lovely day. Couldn't it last just a little
longer?

"Pippa, things have been very strange between us
since you arrived, and I suppose they were bound
to be. But today—it was different—something happened between us."

"Something happened between the boy and girl
we were pretending to be, but that doesn't really
count."

"It could if we wanted it to," he murmured,
brushing her forehead with his lips. "Don't you
want to?"

"No, I...I don't—"

His lips were caressing her cheek, her jaw. "Do
you really mean that?"

"I don't know, but you're not being fair. Please,
Luke, let me go. It's been lovely, but now we have
to be sensible."

"Sensible?" he whispered against her mouth.
"Us?"

"Yes—us," she whispered back. She couldn't resist softly touching his hair, wanting him even as
she denied him. And the yearning little voice inside
cried, "Just this once."

"No!" she said in alarm, pulling herself free of
him. Trembling she turned to face him, seeing his
shocked face, fighting not to let her feelings run
away with her.

"I'm sorry, Luke, but can't you see it's too late?
We can't put the clock back. We pretended for a
day, and it was wonderful, but it's over now, and
this is reality."

"Reality." Luke gave a grunt of mirthless laughter. "How I always hated that word."

"Yes, me, too, sometimes. And this is one of them."

"Then—"

"Darling, please. Everything's different. *I'm* different." She gave a wan smile. "I grew up and became sensible. I'm afraid there's no getting rid of it now."

"No," he said heavily. "I guess not. I'm sorry, Pippa, I guess I misunderstood—a lot of things." He seemed to pull himself together. "You're right of course. We can't put the clock back. I was out of line. Forget it. I'll make you that tea. I'm famous for my English tea."

He was smiling, almost clowning again, declaring the subject closed. She matched his smile with her own, and the dangerous moment passed. As soon as she could she took the tea he made her, bade him good-night and went to her room. Luckily Josie was asleep, and she was free to lie silently in bed, aching with longing and sadness. She would have been a fool to yield to Luke and her own heart, but as she stared into the darkness she was calling herself all kinds of a fool for not being a fool.

Luke didn't go to bed. He did what he often did, went to lie stretched out on the sofa, watching the darkness. Sometimes he would stay there all night, waiting for the first touch of gray in the sky, the first glint on the sea. And it was here that he embarked on the process that passed, with him, for thinking.

It had alarmed and disconcerted him to discover that he wanted Pippa as much as he ever had. This had simply never happened before. "There's nothing so dead as a dead love," ran the saying, and while he had sometimes returned to the bed of a previous lover, it had always been an exercise in nostalgia. What he felt now wasn't nostalgia but the sharp edge of desire. As badly as he'd ever wanted anything in his life he wanted to take Pippa to his room, undress her and himself and make love to her until they were both exhausted. And then he wanted to make love to her again.

He remembered some of the little teasing entice- ments she'd known by instinct and used without mercy. How he'd loved them then and how he ached for them now. He smiled, but in the same moment his body began to respond to the memories, and he forced himself to suppress them. A man couldn't afford to think like that about a woman who'd re- jected him. It made life too difficult.

Pippa had rejected him.

But this was a new and unknown woman whose mystery still held promise.

Not the Pippa of the past, but a different person, part known, part stranger, wholly tantalizing. Young Pippa had been joined by grown-up Pippa, sensible Pippa and even sad Pippa. He didn't know what had made him think of that, but he saw her in his mind, looking pensive, as though she concealed some in- ner pain. And now he realized how often her face wore that look.

He dozed for a while, was awakened by a noise from the kitchen and went to investigate.

"It's only me, Daddy. I'm getting some milk."

"It's four in the morning. You ought to be out like a light after the day you had. Want something to eat?"

"Ice cream?"

"God bless your stomach!" Luke said fervently. "Ice cream, after candy floss, toffee apple—here."

"Thanks."

He sat on the bar stool and watched her eat. "What's it like living in the guest house, Josie?"

"Nice. Mommy said you used to live there with her."

"Yes, but that was a while back. I expect it's changed."

"It's been done up. It's all bright and cheerful now. Would you like to see? I've got some pictures. Hang on."

She slid quietly back up to the bedroom and returned a moment later with a wad of pictures.

"Mommy brought some, too," she said, climbing back onto the stool, "but I don't know where hers are."

Luke studied the house, which had indeed been transformed, especially the kitchen. Ma's kitchen, he recalled, had been fit only for a museum.

"Who's that?" he asked suddenly, pointing to a man standing with Pippa. They were raising their glasses to each other.

"That's Derek. He's in love with Mommy. He keeps giving her roses. Look, you can see them just behind Mommy's shoulder."

Peering closely, Luke made out a bunch of vivid red roses. He said nothing.

"And this one's Mark," Josie said, pressing another photograph in his hand. "He tests cars for a manufacturer, and he does some racing, only Formula Three, though. He takes Mommy out sometimes and drives her really fast. She likes it. She says it's exciting. Funny."

"Why is it funny?"

"Well, she's Mommy. Somehow you don't think of your mother finding things exciting."

"She wasn't always your mother. When I knew her she found everything exciting."

"What was she like then?"

"Fun," he said with a little smile. "She wore these crazy clothes, orange jeans and purple cowboy boots."

"Mom?" Josie said sceptically. "Sure you haven't confused her with another girlfriend?"

"Watch it, smarty! Anyway, I didn't have any other girlfriends when I was with her. Somehow, when Pippa was around you never saw anyone else. She just lit up the sky and made all the world as crazy and wonderful as she was."

He saw Josie's puzzled look and realized that his words made no sense to her. She couldn't relate them to her mother.

"She certainly seems cheerful enough in this one," he said, returning to the photos.

Pippa was sitting in an open-topped car, her hair windblown, her face smiling. Beside her sat a man Luke supposed women would have called handsome. He didn't know. There was no accounting for tastes. He handed the picture back.

"And how does Mommy feel?" he asked. "Does she have any special friends?"

"You mean, anyone who stays all night in her room?" Josie asked wisely.

He felt himself reddening. "Um…yes, I suppose I mean that."

"Don't think so. I never hear any moaning and groaning."

"What…what do you know about moaning and groaning?" he demanded, aghast.

"We had a honeymoon couple once, and they—"

"Yes, all right," he said hastily, adding in a mutter, "Good grief, if I'd said anything like that to my mother she'd have fainted."

"It's a new generation, Dad. Things have changed since your day."

"Get back to bed. You're making me feel ancient."

"Well, face it, Dad. You *were* born in the last century."

He was definitely slipping. She'd vanished before he thought to say, "So were you!"

When she'd gone he looked at the photos again, wishing the man in the car hadn't been so good-looking, and wondering if he had anything to do with Pippa's rejection of himself. He returned to the front room and sat in darkness, looking out over the sea, trying to shake off a gnawing sadness. It was a feeling he never wasted much time on. If something made him sad, he turned his thoughts in a different direction. But it wasn't so easy this time, and he, the least analytical of men, was being forced to analyze.

It had to do with Josie's bewilderment as he described the young Pippa. To her it had simply been gibberish. She was ten, an age when people stayed in their pigeonholes, and Pippa's pigeonhole was "Mom," a sedate woman with headaches and asthma, who told her when to go to bed and often said no. Luke's memories of the bright, beautiful peacock who laughed and squabbled and lived only

for the moment when she could fly into his arms would have no meaning for her.

That young girl was fast slipping away. Pippa herself didn't seem to remember much about her. It was only in his own heart that she still lived, flaming with joy and life and making the world a thrilling place.

But he, too, had changed. What had he said on the boat that afternoon? That their blazing sexual harmony had mattered less, in the long term, than the fact that their minds were in tune. He, Luke Danton, superstud extraordinary, had actually said that.

And meant it. Scary!

It was the sort of thing boring Frank might have said, and that alarmed Luke more than anything. It meant he was growing old.

Or up?

He rubbed his eyes, wishing he hadn't start thinking. It made him feel like a bear fending off a swarm of bees, and gave him a headache.

The program went on at eight o'clock in the evening. By five the entire family was in place, consisting of Mom, Pop, Zak and his girlfriend, Becky and her boyfriend. Half an hour later Claudia arrived bearing vintage champagne, and the party was complete.

Luke had outdone himself with supper, preparing one main course and a host of small savories that could be eaten at any time. Josie, who liked nothing better than to be her father's assistant, scurried about performing her tasks efficiently and glowing when she won a word of praise from the boss.

Luke smiled at Pippa, but he didn't ask her to

help. She wondered if this was because he was at ease with his daughter in his kitchen as he was with nobody else. Or was he keeping a distance because of last night? It was hard to tell because his manner was friendly, if preoccupied.

By 7:45 the curtains were drawn over the picture window, the VCR was set to record, and everyone was settled in the main room. With a flourish Luke switched on the television, and they sat in an agony of impatience while the last program finished and the ads dragged by.

"This is it," Luke declared confidently.

But another advertisement came on, and everybody booed. Then the program started, and they all sat in awed silence, the only sound being a long, ecstatic sigh from Josie. When it was over they applauded, and Luke ceremonially presented his daughter with the video.

"I'll have it copied to the European video system before you leave," he said. "But this one's in case you wanted to see it again before then."

"Leave!" Mom said, outraged. "What's this talk of leaving?"

"We're only here for a week," Pippa explained, "and it'll soon be over."

There was a general outcry. She coped with it as best she could, but as soon as possible she escaped into the kitchen. Her breath was coming in short gasps, and she felt faint.

Claudia found her there a few moments later. "Are you all right?" she asked solicitously.

"Yes, fine. Just a touch of asthma, it gets me sometimes. I was a bit nervous about coming to Los Angeles—everyone's heard of the smog."

"Sure. Although this part of L.A. is one of the cleanest. Very little air pollution around here."

"Well, I guess I'm just unusually susceptible." Pippa smiled valiantly. "Let's go back to the others."

Pippa could recall vacations as a child when the week ahead had seemed to stretch to infinity and had gone on doing so until the halfway mark. But once that was passed every day sped by like lightning.

Now it was the same. After the night of the program the few remaining days blurred into each other, and only odd moments stood out: Josie and Luke investigating the Web site that was deluged with complimentary e-mails following the broadcast; Josie being swept off to Disneyland again by Luke's parents. She'd stayed at home resting that morning, joining Luke at his first restaurant for lunch. He'd dined her royally, given her the grand tour of the kitchens and attended to her comfort and pleasure. But there was a shadow in his manner that hadn't been there before, and her heart sank as she understood. He had accepted her decision and would let her go with only a little regret. It was Josie he would keep in touch with, Josie he would visit and invite to visit him. And that was how she had wanted it.

The other moment that lived in her memory was a late afternoon, when she'd gone out onto the balcony to watch for Luke and Josie, who were out in the water, enjoying a final romp before the day ended. The sun was setting, casting a flood of gold over the sea and the sand, throwing the figures into

silhouette. There was Luke, in the water up to his waist. As Pippa watched, he ducked down far enough for Josie to clamber onto his shoulders. Reaching over his head and behind he grasped her by the hips and raised her high, while she stretched out her arms and her legs, as though flying. He began to turn around and around. Josie's head was back, and even from this distance Pippa could see that she was ecstatic.

Then the whole thing collapsed. Luke took a big jump and tossed Josie forward so that she landed in the water at the same time as he crashed back into it himself. For a moment they were drowned in spray. Then they both came up, laughing—no, Pippa amended…giggling. Both of them. A pair of mad things, as her mother used to say.

That's just how a father and daughter ought to be, she thought. A pair of mad things. Happy just to be together. And in the years ahead—

Suddenly she felt as though she'd crashed against a wall made of black ice—the years ahead—which she would probably know nothing about. And with a passionate intensity that was painful, she wished she could be there for them. She wanted to see Luke at his daughter's graduation, proud to bursting. She wanted to see him take her up the aisle on his arm and wipe his eyes as another man led her away.

She wanted the funny things, too: Luke, outside a maternity ward muttering, "I'm a grandfather. She can't *do* this to me!" But then being struck dumb at the sight of the little scrap, and perhaps calling it Josie by mistake, because that was when he would really care about the years he'd missed.

It would happen. Whatever the big occasions of

Josie's life, Luke would be there. She had made sure of that. But she might never know. And suddenly the scene blurred. She couldn't see anymore. Turning, she blundered back inside.

Luke and Josie returned to find the house empty. She'd gone for a walk, she told them when she returned. Just a walk, and she was fine. No, honestly. Fine.

The last two days, the last day, the last hours on the beach with Luke and his mom and dad and Zak and Claudia. Nobody wanted to be left out. Pippa couldn't remember when she'd last been so totally surrounded by kindness and affection.

Several times she surprised a puzzled look in Josie's eyes, and once the child said, "Mommy, are you and Daddy going to get back together?"

"No, darling."

"But you love each other."

"We're very fond of each other, but only as friends now."

"But—"

"Darling, leave it there, please. And don't say anything to Daddy. One day you'll understand."

And Josie had come as close as she ever had to sulking. "I hate it when you say that."

That brief conversation had been more of a strain on Pippa than she wanted to admit. She knew that from now on—whatever happened—she could be sure Luke would insist on being Josie's father. But nothing else had gone according to plan. She'd meant to establish friendly relations with Luke, but not to let herself fall in love with him again. Now she saw how unrealistic that had been. After all this time, she still couldn't be near him without her heart warming to him, and she ought to have known that, she thought ruefully.

She'd come to the brink of falling in love with him again, but only the brink, she assured herself. There was still time to recover, when there was a safe distance between them. But what really troubled her was the fact that she still hadn't told him the real reason she'd come here. She'd always imagined that the chance would present itself and she would seize it.

But somehow the time had never quite been right, and now it was the last day, the last few moments. "Have we got all your bags, Pippa? What about that one?" Packing the last few things away, a tight fit. A look around the kitchen, imprinting it on her memory. Luke, watching her, half smiling, half baffled, almost the same frown in his eyes as in Josie's.

They went to the airport in procession. Claudia drove the first car, with Luke and Pippa and Zak. His mom, dad and Becky brought up the rear with Josie, all caroling songs at the top of their voices.

"You've got a bit of time," Dad announced once Pippa had checked in and seen the bags on their way. "How about a chocolate sundae?"

"Please, Mommy," Josie begged, seeing caution on her mother's face.

Zak put his hand on her shoulder. "C'mon, little one."

Here was her moment alone with Luke, and now she wished she'd never had it. For she'd been through this before, the last few minutes before departure, telling herself to keep a stiff upper lip just a little longer, not to let him suspect that her heart was breaking. That time he'd been the one going away.

"Well," she said brightly, "this is it."

"Yes, I guess it—" Suddenly Luke grasped her arm. "Come with me," he said firmly. "We have to talk."

He drew her firmly around a corner so that they were out of sight of the others. "This is all wrong," he said. "I can't let it happen."

"Luke—what?"

"You can't go. I won't let you. No, listen—" he interrupted her before she could say a word. "Don't you see, this is what happened before—when I left England? *And I shouldn't have gone.* I was crazy about you, and I walked away from it, but I shouldn't have. Pippa, didn't you feel that at the time? I can't believe you didn't."

"I—you—it was your decision to go. You didn't have to."

"I know. My decision. But it was the wrong one, for both of us. It wouldn't have taken much to make me stay. But you were so matter-of-fact, joking about me flirting with other women on the plane. I couldn't tell what you felt, if anything. We'd been so much to each other, and you waved me off with a laugh."

She could only stare at him, dumbstruck.

"Pippa, I never told you this, but when I reached the departure lounge I came to a dead halt. My feet wouldn't go any farther. I didn't want to get on that plane."

"You didn't?"

"It was wrong for me to go then, and it's wrong for you to go now. I won't let you go, Pippa. It's no use arguing. No!'' He slapped his forehead. ''No, that's all wrong. I'm making a mess of this.'' He was talking very fast. ''I just want you to stay for another week—or two—so that I can persuade you. Yes, that's better. Persuade. That's what I should have said to start with.''

''You're babbling.''

''Am I? Yes, I am. You know why? Because if I stop talking you'll give me an answer and I'm afraid of it. Just another two weeks—or three—''

''But—''

''You can't go like this. It's too soon. Josie doesn't want to go. She wants to stay here and move into Disneyland with Dad. I don't want you to go. Mom and Dad don't want you to go. Pippa, please say *you* don't want to go.''

''Luke—''

''No, wait a minute, don't rush to answer. Stop and think about it. If you just stay a little longer, three weeks—or maybe four—''

She couldn't speak for happiness. This was what she had dreamed of years ago, Luke begging, pleading with her to stay with him. It had happened at last. But it was all wrong. It had come too late, and now she must tell him what she'd ducked out of telling him before.

''Darling—''

''Say it again. Let me hear you call me darling.''

''Darling Luke, please—there's something I—''

''Just one more week, Pippa, and I swear I won't ask for more—well, maybe two. We have so much to talk about, and it can't be done at a distance.''

Happy as she was, she knew a little spurt of anger.

It had been done at a distance when it suited him. "There's the phone, and the e-mail—" she began to say.

"But it's different now, don't you know that? Something started to happen between us—I know you're denying it, and maybe I know why, but give me a chance. Don't throw away what we could have."

Pippa stared, hardly able to believe her ears, while the spurt of anger leaped higher. It was different now that *he* wanted it to be different.

Stop it, said an inner voice. *It doesn't matter anymore, and you can't quarrel with him here and now.*

But the old, pugnacious Pippa reared her head, yelling, *I can quarrel with him anyplace and anytime I like.*

"This is the first call for British Airways Flight 1083, Los Angeles to London Heathrow..."

He seized her arms. "You're not taking that plane."

"You bet I'm not," she said slowly. "You're right. There are things to say, and I'm going to stay right here and say them."

His heart leaped. He'd won. Of course he had. He always did. But there was something in her eyes that made him uneasy. It should have been the light of love. It looked more like the light of battle. Being Luke, he brushed it aside to be worried about later.

He took her hand firmly, and they returned to the café. Everyone stopped and looked up at them eagerly. "Who's going to get their bags off the flight?" Luke asked, and a cheer went up.

Josie cast herself wildly against Pippa. *"Thank*

you, Mommy!'' Then against Luke, who held her tight.

Zak went off to recover the bags. Luke's mother seized Pippa's hand and pulled her down beside her.

"We've had this wonderful idea," she said. "Why don't you let Josie stay with us for a while?"

"No, I'm sorry," Pippa said at once. "That's out of the question."

They stared at her, everyone taken aback.

"Forgive me. I didn't mean to be rude. Of course I know you'll take wonderful care of her. It's just that she's never been out of my sight before."

But very soon, you may be out of each other's sight forever. Put the thought aside. Don't look at it. But bind her tightly to those who love her.

"Please, Mommy," Josie begged. "Grandpa says we'll go to Disneyland every day."

"He's never had an excuse as good as this before," his wife put in.

"Well," Pippa said helplessly, "I guess maybe...a few days—"

This cheer was even louder than the other, making passersby cover their ears.

"When Zak brings the baggage, we'll just load Josie's things in our car and head for home," Luke's dad declared.

"You mean now?" Pippa asked.

"Guess there's no time like the present."

"Guess there isn't, at that," Pippa said, dazed. She felt as though she'd been squashed by a friendly but determined juggernaut. They were all in it. Except perhaps Claudia.

And a few minutes later even that illusion was destroyed.

* * *

"Hey, this isn't the way back to Manhattan Beach," Pippa said, looking around her, puzzled.

They were in Claudia's car and she was driving them home, so she'd claimed. "I thought we'd do a little detour," she said airily over her shoulder.

"How big a detour?"

"Montecito, just southeast of Santa Barbara. I have a little house there, and while Josie stays with Luke's family, you'll stay with me."

"But—"

"You'll love it, Pippa. The air is cooler and cleaner than Los Angeles. That'll suit you better."

Pippa whirled on Luke who was sitting beside her in the back seat.

"Don't look at me," he said with suspicious innocence. "I've been kidnapped, too."

"There's kidnapping," Pippa said emphatically, "and kidnapping!"

"Darn! I was afraid you'd spot that one."

"Luke, you can't just sweep me off like that."

His face was full of wicked fun. "I'm not. She is."

"But—"

He slipped both arms about her, drawing her back onto the seat beside him. "Why don't you just lie back and enjoy it?"

She couldn't struggle anymore. He was irresistible, thank goodness! And why should she even think of struggling against something she so passionately wanted? Pippa slid down into the seat and gave herself up to Luke's embrace.

She spared a last conscience-stricken thought for Claudia, reduced to playing gooseberry in her own car. But from somewhere in the distance she heard a delighted chuckle and guessed Claudia had peeked in her rearview mirror.

They drove for nearly two hours. Then they were climbing into the hills, and, as Claudia had promised, she could feel the air growing cooler and fresher. She took a long breath of pure physical joy. In the distance the ocean sparkled. Above, the sky gleamed an impossible blue.

Suddenly Claudia took a turn that had been invisible. Another mile, driving amidst lush vegetation, and her house came into view. Pippa stared, openmouthed. Luke had said that Claudia's wealth came from oil, and now she knew it must be true.

The house was a low, rambling Spanish-style edifice—white walls, red tile roof. For a while it came and went between the trees, but then suddenly the trees cleared and it was before them like a vision.

Claudia stopped the car, tooting cheerfully, and bringing two men and two women bustling out of the house. "Sonia, Catalina, Ruiz and Alfonso," she said. "They look after the house and garden."

In moments Ruiz and Alfonso had opened the trunk to remove all the baggage, Sonia and Catalina were ushering them into the house, welcoming them volubly, assuring them that everything was prepared, the rooms were ready, the food was laid out.

Inside, the air was blessedly cool. Long white curtains wafted gently in the floor-to-ceiling windows.

Claudia escorted Pippa upstairs to a room at the front of the house.

"This is yours," she said. "Luke's is across the way."

The room, which matched the one directly below, was big enough for ten. It had floor-to-ceiling windows, hung with white net curtains, and mosaic tiles on the floor. Its high ceiling and wide spaces gave it an air of peace that seemed to bless her as soon as she walked in. The bed, which could have slept an army, was covered in white lace. The furniture was rosewood, warm, glowing and beautiful.

Catalina was already there, unpacking Pippa's clothes and hanging them in the huge closets. She showed her where everything was, smiled and disappeared.

Pippa wandered out onto the wrought-iron balcony to stand looking over the pool and beyond it the sea, feeling all the troubles fall away from her soul.

"Do you like it?" Claudia asked from the doorway.

"Claudia, it's beautiful."

"It's my room. I chose it because it overlooks the sea."

"But I can't drive you out of your room. I'll take somewhere else."

"Oh, but I won't be here. I have to dash off for a few days. Did I forget to mention it?"

"Yes, you somehow forgot that," Pippa said.

"Well, I have a memory like a sieve," Claudia declared gaily. "I forgot to mention this, too."

On the bed lay a robe of pure silk, multi-colored in shades of olive-green, tan, orange, pale-yellow. It was the most exquisite thing Pippa had ever seen.

"It's an old Spanish custom to make a gift when someone stays in your house," Claudia said. "This is my gift. It's for lying around by the pool."

She held it up, and it looked so perfect that Pippa gasped with pleasure. "It looks fantastic with your

coloring,'' Claudia said. "I'm rather conceited with myself for getting that so right.''

"Claudia it's—it's—''

"Oh, hush, it's nothing. Just enjoy it.'' Then abruptly the gaiety faded from her face, and she spoke quietly. "You probably wonder why I brought you here, when you and Luke could simply have returned to his house. But I thought you needed to get away completely. It's all been about Luke and Josie, but what about Luke and you?''

"I'm not sure that there can be a Luke and me.''

"Now you can find out. And I want you to take this.'' She handed Pippa a scrap of paper on which a name and address were written. "He's my own doctor here and he knows how to be discreet.''

"I don't know what you—'' Pippa began quickly, but her protests died under the gentle honesty on Claudia's face.

"I don't know what it is exactly,'' Claudia said. "But I know there's something, and you haven't told Luke. Maybe you'll tell him while you're here. I think it should be soon.''

Pippa looked down at the paper in her hand. "Thank you,'' she said quietly. "You won't—''

"No, I won't interfere. Besides, I'll be gone in a few minutes.''

Impulsively she put her hands on Pippa's shoulder and kissed her on the cheek. Pippa clung to her for a moment, smiling. Suddenly she felt full of courage. She would tell Luke without delay.

Chapter Nine

Claudia whisked herself out of the house with very little fuss. She stopped briefly with Luke to tell him, "If I'm not back to drive you home, just take something from the garage." Then she gave him a hug, said, "Bye, both of you. Don't bother to be good."

"We won't," Luke promised her fervently. And Claudia was gone.

Then an odd thing happened. As Luke and Pippa turned to look at each other a constraint seemed to fall over them. Pippa understood it in herself. She had something momentous to tell him. But Luke seemed actually embarrassed.

Sonia saved them by waddling from the kitchen yodeling, "Food! You come and eat little snacks while I cook big dinner."

"Great," Luke said with evident relief. "Let's have them by the pool."

He vanished upstairs at once, leaving Pippa feeling puzzled. She returned to Claudia's room and put through a call to England.

"Mark, hi! Yes, I know I should be on the plane by now, but we're staying over a few more days. I called so that you'd know not to meet us at the airport." She saw a shadow slip past her half-open door. It was Luke on his way down to the pool. On the other end of the line Mark sounded troubled.

"Pippa, you've got major surgery scheduled for next week—"

"I know, but I can have a few extra days here and still be back in time. I'll call Frank and—"

"No need, he's here. He was going to come to the airport with me. You'd better talk to him."

She heard the mutter of voices, and the next moment there was Frank, sounding outraged and fearful. "You must be out of your mind."

"Frank, I'm feeling really well. Please try to understand."

"Fine, it's plainly useless for me to talk sense to you. I'd like to speak to Josie, please."

"She's not here. She's staying with Luke's parents."

She heard his sharp intake of breath. "So that you can be with *him,* I suppose. He broke your heart once and he'll do it again, but don't you care about that! *Don't you care about anything but your fancy man!*" He slammed down the phone.

Such violence of feeling was so unlike Frank that she could only sigh, pitying him. In many ways she knew he was right. She ought to be strong and say goodbye to Luke. But the happiness that possessed her now was so sweet, and there had been so little of it in her life, that no power on earth could have prevented her claiming just a little more, perhaps the last she would ever know.

She called Luke's parents. Zak answered and said they'd taken Josie to the zoo. He promised to tell Josie that she'd arrived safely, and get her to call when she arrived home.

When she went down, dressed for swimming, with the silk robe over her costume, Luke was already in the water. Sonia was setting out the snacks and wine by the pool.

"Champagne," she said. "Miss Claudia's orders."

"Miss Claudia's really organizing things," Pippa murmured.

"She's like a big sister to Mr. Luke," Sonia confided. "She knows what's good for him."

She poured a champagne into a tall, fluted glass, handed it to Pippa and put the bottle back on ice. Pippa sipped and found herself drinking vintage Krug, chilled to perfection. She slipped off her robe and sat on the side, dangling one foot in the water. It was deliciously cool, and glinted in the sun as though the very water was made of champagne.

"Come on," Luke called from the water. "It's great."

"So's the champagne," she called back.

He swam over to her, threw his head back, mouth open wide. Laughing she poured champagne directly into it. "More! More!" She filled the glass again, but this time she emptied it over his head. *"Hey!"* he spluttered, and vanished beneath the water.

Pippa peered down at him, but the next moment a hand had encircled her ankle and she was in the water with him. He released her at once and carried her to the surface, spluttering and struggling. Pippa found herself pressed against his bare torso, feeling the flesh warm despite the cool water, and suddenly very, very conscious of how much of her own body was uncovered.

"You let me go, right now," she said breathlessly.

To her surprise, he did so, and swam away, leaving her startled.

He shouldn't have left her like that, even if she'd told him to. His hands seemed to have made imprints in her waist where he'd held her, and the sensation of his body against hers was still alive. But he had gone. He was up at the far end of the huge pool, splashing and frolicking as though nothing had happened between them.

She swam lazily, crossing the pool at the width rather than risking the length. She was feeling good, but she knew how quickly that could evaporate.

At last they climbed out and dried themselves off. Luke held up the robe for her to put her arms in. "Pretty," he said. "I haven't seen it before."

"Claudia gave it to me. I feel a fraud, it's such perfect silk, and I'm not really a silk kind of person."

"Why shouldn't you wear the best?" He briefly kissed her cheek and settled down on his own recliner. "Let's eat. It looks good."

The snacks were Spanish *tapas,* small portions of fish, meat and salad, and Sonia, whose family came from Andalucia, had turned them into an art form.

They both enjoyed them with gusto, until Luke said, "Pippa, we have to talk."

"What about?" she asked, puzzled by an edgy note in his voice.

"There's something we should have discussed days ago, but I guess I lost my nerve. You, too, maybe."

"Me...too?"

"Lost your nerve. Because it's something you really should have told me at the start, not let me blunder on, thinking that you—that we—"

He floundered to a halt, and in the silence Pippa felt herself drowning in horror. Luke had guessed the truth about her illness. What else could this mean?

"Luke, please don't blame me too much—"

"I don't. I know some things are hard to say. It's just that you were always such an honest person— well, you'd tell the truth if it brought an avalanche down on you...and on the rest of us."

"Maybe I've learned a little tact," she said quietly. "When you grow up, you don't want to risk avalanches. They tend to engulf the people you love."

"I wish I knew who you include on that list."

"Well...Josie mainly. You must understand that I've had to put her first."

"Of course." He seemed deflated. "It's just— would you tell me whether it's too late?"

Oh, God! He did know.

"I can't tell if it's too late or not," she said slowly. "How can I know that before I've got back to London?"

"And seen him."

"What?"

"Mark. That's his name, isn't it? You called him from your room...."

"Yes, he was due to meet us at the other end. I had to let him know not to."

"You were on the phone to him a long time."

"I called Josie, too, but she was at the zoo." She couldn't mention Frank.

"Is he a nice guy, this Mark?"

"Very nice."

"A good friend?"

"The best."

"Handsome, too."

"Very. In the guest house we call him Adonis."

"Oh, really! Well, I guess that's that! More champagne."

"Luke—what is it?" She dismissed the suspicion creeping into her head as too impossible. "How did you know he was handsome?"

"Josie showed me some snapshots. There was a real nice one of you and him together in his car. She says you go driving with him a lot." He was looking out over the pool.

"Luke is this what you were talking about just now? Mark and me?"

"Of course. What else?"

They'd been at cross-purposes. He hadn't discovered her secret, after all. She could still tell him in her own way.

And now the suspicion became a reality. He was jealous. "So, you put two and two together, and came up with—what?"

"I don't know," he said grumpily. "You tell me. I mean, look—it's fair enough. I guess there was bound to be someone—and you tried to give me a hint—all that stuff about things being different. That's what you meant, wasn't it? About this Mark guy, and his fast cars and his Adonis looks. What's so damned funny?''

"You are," she chuckled. "Making a big deal about Mark.''

"He isn't a big deal?''

"He's no kind of deal. Just a friend. They all are.''

"That wasn't what you were trying to tell me the other night?''

"No, it wasn't. But, Luke, I want to talk to you about something quite different—''

He never heard her. His relief took the form of leaping to his feet, yelling, *"Yahooo!"* at the top of his voice, and toppling headfirst into the pool, landing with a splash that soaked her.

"Yahooo!" he yelled. *"YAHOOO!"*

She knew she should be firm and insist on telling him everything now, but like that other time, the knowledge that he was jealous filled the world. It could do no harm to enjoy her happiness for just a little longer. She would tell him tomorrow.

He swam back to her. "You're not in love with Mark?'' he yelled.

She knelt down to talk to him. "No, of course I'm not.''

"You're not in love with anyone else?''

"No!"

"YAHOOO!" Pippa covered her ears, laughing. "Listen—'' he yelled. She uncovered them. "What did you think I meant, then?''

"Pardon?''

"You said I shouldn't blame you. Blame you for what? What did you think I meant?"

Her mind went blank. "I didn't know what you meant," she prevaricated. "I thought you were talking gibberish, the way you usually do. I just played along."

"But you must have meant something when you said—"

Inspiration came to her. "What's that?" she called, leaning down to him. "I can't hear you."

"I said—*aaaaauuurgh!*"

The last sound was a yell that became a gurgle as Pippa "lost her balance" and toppled into the water, contriving to land neatly on top of him. They both sank into the depths and came up laughing. Pippa turned and swam away from him toward the shallow end where a brief flight of steps led up to the pool deck. She skipped up them, but they were slippery and she missed her footing, falling onto one knee.

"Darling!" He caught her in time to prevent her going down any farther. "Are you all right?"

"I'm fine—that is—my knee took a bit of a bang. Just help me sit down."

He did so, tenderly wrapping a towel robe around her, lifting her legs onto the recliner and gently rubbing her knee until she pronounced that it was better. By that time, she was relieved to see, he'd forgotten what he'd been trying to ask her.

She was succumbing to an attack of blissful madness. It might be wrong, and sometime soon there would be a reckoning, but she would seize what life had offered her and count the cost later. Only a short time ago she'd been a sad creature, facing a return to the wilderness where there was no Luke, where she might never see him again. Suddenly all sadness was swept away. Before her stretched blissful days, and when the clock struck twelve, Cinderella wouldn't complain.

"What is it?" he asked quickly.

"What?"

"You sighed."

"Did I? I didn't know."

"Let me pour you some more champagne. Then you can tell me what you'd like to do for the rest of the day."

"Well, first I'll drink the champagne, and then—" she stretched and yawned "—then I'll let you pour me some more champagne."

"Yes, ma'am."

"After that I think I'll take a nap. It's been a tiring week, and now that I'm a lady of leisure I'm going to make the most of it. When I wake up I'll have a long, luxurious bath."

"By which time supper will be ready."

"Hey, what are you doing?"

"Carrying you, so that you don't have to put too much pressure on that knee."

"Oh, yes, my knee," she said vaguely, trying to remember which knee he was talking about.

On the way into the house Luke said something in Spanish to Sonia, who bustled away. As they reached the top of the stairs, she was already in Pippa's room, turning down the bed.

"Shoo," Luke said, when Sonia showed a disposition to linger.

"And you can shoo, as well," Pippa said as he set her down. "I'm going to have a long sleep."

"Can't I stay?"

"No," she said firmly.

He smiled and began to help her off with the towel robe. And from nowhere came that little spurt of resentment she'd felt at the airport. He was so assured.

"Goodbye, Luke," she said.

He smiled and kissed the end of her nose. "You don't mean that. Think how well I could help you to sleep!"

"If I swing my fist, you'll be the one who goes to sleep—for twenty-four hours," she teased. "Now go."

"All right," he laughed. "Have a nice snooze, darling." He blew her a kiss and departed.

She slid down blissfully into Claudia's bed, wondering what had come over her to be so perverse. It was only half an hour ago she'd been happy just to be with Luke, longing for him. But he knew it and took it for granted just a little too much. And why shouldn't he? Nobody had ever said no to Luke.

But *you* did, said a perverse voice in her head. Since you arrived in Los Angeles a week ago, Luke has let you know in several ways that he still desires you, and you've turned him down.

So he kidnapped you. He virtually admitted it and expected you to see it his way. Things happen when it suits him, and only when it suits him. He was disconcerted about Mark, but only for a moment. He didn't really believe life could go against him. And now he thinks all he has to do is make his move.

He'll seduce you with teasing affection, delicately, subtly, making sure that you love every moment, for your pleasure will be as important to him as his own. That's what makes him so dangerously charming. But the end result will be what it always is. Luke will get his own way.

The clouds began to roll over her mind. She couldn't think of this anymore. She was too comfortable. Bidding the voice be silent, she slept.

She awoke to the sound of a bath being run. Sonia looked in, beamed and held up the robe for her to get into.

The bathroom was an eye-opener. Claudia had fancied the idea of a Greek temple, and her designer had gone to town. The bath was sunk in the floor and decorated with jigsaw mosaic around the rim. Elegant mosaics covered the walls. Sonia poured something into the water, and a delicious aroma assailed Pippa's nostrils.

She stepped into the scented water, feeling her cares vanish. To her relief the awkward voice was silent, and she was once more full of goodwill toward Luke.

She owned one good evening dress in a soft, green material that she wore with gilt accessories. Sonia then revealed that she'd once worked in a beauty parlor, and took over the management of her hair, brushing and curling it into an enchanting arrangement on top of her head.

Luke *was* enchanted. It was in his appraisal as she descended the stairs and took his outstretched hand. His eyes were warm and caressing, paying her silent tribute.

Because he thinks it's all so easy. The awkward voice was back.

Shut up! she told it firmly. I'm going to enjoy myself tonight.

Darkness had fallen and they dined by candlelight. It was Sonia's proud boast that she was the only person who could cook for Luke without reducing him to a nervous wreck, and Pippa soon found how she'd earned her reputation. The food was perfect. The wine was perfect. The atmosphere was perfect. Everything was perfect.

Too perfect. The voice again. It couldn't be silenced because it came from part of her own mind, the part that was still set to Common Sense. This section had several buttons of varying degrees of intensity, ranging from Oh, Yeah! through Pull the Other One! to Don't Take Me for a Fool! Right this minute Luke was racing up the scale with alarming speed, but she made a determined effort not to get upset. She really wanted to enjoy herself.

"I adore our daughter," he said as he refilled her wineglass. "But if you were to ask me if I mind that she's in someone else's care tonight," he held up his hand, "I cannot tell a lie. I'm delighted."

"I am, too," Pippa admitted. She took a mouthful of the confection Sonia had set before her. It was made of cream and ice cream, covered in a sauce made with wine, and she made a face of bliss.

"It's mind-blowing, isn't it?" Luke agreed. "I keep begging Sonia for the recipe, but she's holding out on me. Her best offer is to leave it to me in her will. Have some of mine, it's slightly different from yours."

They exchanged spoonfuls.

"Why are you looking at me like that?" she asked.

"Just thinking how gorgeous you look in the candlelight."

It was wonderful, he thought, how the years had

changed her from a delightful girl to a spell-binding woman. Attractive had turned into beautiful, funny had become mysterious, and cheekily sexy was now sexually alluring. He was in a fever to make love with her. When their fingers touched over the spoons he felt a jolt of electricity that radiated over his skin until it homed in on his loins. He put his spoon down with a clatter and took a deep breath to steady himself. This wasn't easy.

They had a ten-year-old child, for Pete's sake, and he was trembling like a boy who'd never been to bed before. The thought of the coming night made him smile, adoring her.

"Come and look at the moon," he said, wondering how much more waiting he could stand. He took her hand and drew her to the French doors. A subtle perfume came from her body as she walked, and the light played on her bare shoulders, making the temptation to touch them irresistible.

His lips followed his hands, tracing gentle patterns on her bare skin, while his fingers glided along her arms.

"Luke—" To her dismay her response was dead.

"Sweet Pippa," he whispered, "kiss me, my love."

He pulled her around and took her into his arms in a deep, passionate embrace.

And she froze.

She couldn't help it.

"What is it?" he murmured against her lips. "Kiss me."

"Luke—let me go—"

He did, but only a little. "Darling, what is it? You've been in a funny mood all evening."

"Have I?"

"Yes, and I thought everything between us was perfect again."

"Everything was never perfect between us, Luke," she said in a calm voice that had a dangerous edge.

He heard it and felt a moment's alarm but no comprehension. "What do you mean? Wasn't it perfect all those years ago?"

"For you maybe, but I got my heart broken."

He frowned. "What do you mean?"

His honest incomprehension was like a match to gunpowder. Suddenly the years rolled back and she was Pippa again, young, pugnacious Pippa, who would as soon quarrel with a man as love him, and quarrel with him the more fiercely for loving him. She broke free and turned her back on the alluring moonlight, walking firmly back into the room.

"I mean—I mean—well, I suppose I mean all those things you were saying at the airport today. All about how we couldn't communicate at a distance. That's what we did for years when you wanted to. Now you've decided otherwise, and instead of doing what I planned, I end up here."

"But, darling, you couldn't have just walked out on me."

"You walked out on me!"

There, she'd said it, after eleven years.

He stared as if she'd said something in another language. "Only because you let me," he said at last.

"You what? I did not 'let' you, you wanted to go."

"You could have stopped me with a word. In fact,

you could have stopped me by just staying there for five minutes. I told you I couldn't go any farther. What I didn't say was that I came all the way back to the barrier. I was so sure you'd still be there, and if you had been I'd have stayed. But not you. You walked straight off the minute I was out of sight. Out of sight, out of mind, huh?''

She stared at him, aghast. It couldn't be true, because if it was true it was unbearable.

''No,'' she said, ''I don't believe that.''

''Hey, c'mon, when have I ever been a liar? I went back, and you weren't there.''

''That's right, I wasn't there,'' she said, breathing hard. ''And you know why? Because you'd made it so clear that you were only around for a short time. Right from the start you were honest. You arranged everything so that I couldn't complain, *because you'd been so bloody honest.*''

He'd never heard her swear before, and it shocked him so much that he could only stare at her, dumbfounded. He didn't know this woman whose face was distorted with anger and unshed tears.

''So I didn't complain. I did everything the way you wanted, the way everyone always does. I smiled and I didn't tell you my heart was breaking at losing you, and breaking again because you were so glad to be going.''

''I wasn't—''

''Shut up! Just for once I'm going to tell you how I really feel about something. This time I'm not pretending in case the truth drives you away. I'm telling you about *my* feelings, what I want, and if you don't like it, then tough! I've spent too long loving you on your terms with nothing back, and I'm fed up.

You didn't want any ties, so I didn't create any, and that's been fine for you. But where did it leave me? Bringing up our child alone in a boarding house *where nobody eats anything but chips.*

"Oh, yes, you've been wonderful about money and you've stayed in touch, after a fashion. I tried to tell myself how lucky I was, because other men don't pay a penny, or they pretend the child isn't theirs. I wouldn't let myself face how selfish you were really being, because money's easy. You're a generous man, as long as it's only money, but ask you to give part of yourself, and you don't want to know.

"And those charming e-mails you and Josie exchange. Anyone can be charming at a distance. Five thousand miles, and switch the machine off when it suits you."

By now Luke had stopped even trying to reply. The world was collapsing around his ears, but that didn't matter. What mattered was that she was in anguish and it was somehow his fault.

She was gasping as though she'd been running, and the words seemed to have run down. She brushed a hand across her face, trying to hide the wetness on her cheeks. Her lips trembled, but he saw her swallow hard and force back the emotion.

"Oh, forget it," she said tiredly.

"No, I think you should say the rest of it, whatever the rest is. I guess there are some things in there that you've been waiting to say for years."

"Yes, well, I thought I wanted to say them, but the time is past. What difference can it make now?"

He poured himself a brandy and offered her one. She took it in one gulp. "Say it," he repeated.

"You'd got as far as switching off the machine when it suited me."

"Well, it's true, isn't it? I've had no machine to switch off. I'm there twenty-four hours a day, because that's what being a parent is. It's not just picking the nice bits. It's the boring bits, reading the same story for the fiftieth time because it's her favorite. It's broken nights, and not being able to go out with your friends because she needs you, and always thinking of her first. Things you wouldn't know anything about.

"It's not just giving her presents and being told you're wonderful. Sometimes it's being told you're horrible because you've said no to something she desperately wanted. You couldn't stand being told you're horrible."

"I'm getting a taste of it now," he said wryly.

"No, you're not horrible. You're selfish and immature and you've got enough charm to make people let you get away with it, so you know nothing about real life. But you're not horrible. That's why I've never said all this before. And maybe I should have done."

"So why didn't you?"

"Because I was young and stupid and so much in love with you that it hurt. I longed to marry you, but I knew that word was like a red rag to a bull. That's why I didn't ask you to Frank and Elly's wedding. I was so scared of losing you, and too ignorant to ask myself if you were worth keeping."

"Thanks!" he said, really nettled now.

"Anyone who's only interested in what he can have on his own terms isn't worth the heartbreak.

And I could have saved myself a lot of pain if I'd seen that before.''

Luke tore his hair. ''I wish I knew where all this came from. A few minutes ago everything was fine—''

''No, everything wasn't fine, not for me. I tried to believe it was, because it was so nice to be playing at romance and having you make a fuss of me. But the truth is that everything hasn't been fine for eleven years.''

''You've felt like this for eleven years?'' he echoed, aghast.

''That surprises you, doesn't it? That really surprises you.''

''But I thought you were okay about it.''

''You thought what you wanted to think. Did you ever once bother to come over to England and see how I was managing?''

''You could have called or written—'' He saw her murderous expression and backtracked hastily. ''No, no, forget I said that.''

''For your sake, yes, I will forget it—just as you forgot me, until now it suits you to remember me again, and I'm supposed to jump into your arms. But I've moved on. I've had a child, and helping her grow up has made *me* grow up.''

''Pippa, please, can't we talk about this calmly?''

''I don't want to talk about it calmly. I want to shout and scream because then maybe you'll understand what you did. I can live with you not bothering about me. What I can't forgive you for is ignoring Josie and thinking you could be a good father at a distance—sending her e-mails and gifts that somebody else picked out, and believing— My God! You really believed that was all there was to it. I shouldn't have had to bring her over here when it's almost too late for me, and if you'd been a half-decent father I wouldn't have had to.''

Luke had paled—the only sign that his rarely aroused temper had begun to flare. ''I suppose I should be glad that you said all this now,'' he said harshly. ''Think how much longer we might have wasted. I've been fooling myself. I'm sorry. I know I was wrong in the past, but I thought I had a chance to make it right between us.''

''Well you haven't,'' she cried. ''It's too late! Years too late. How dare you do this to me now! Go to blazes, Luke! Go to perdition! Go to hell! *I wish I'd never met you.*''

Chapter Ten

Lying alone in bed that night, Pippa could have wept with frustration. Why had she let her temper get the better of her, and spoiled what might have been so beautiful? All she'd had to do was keep quiet.

But when had she ever been able to do that?

It had been so perfect. He was jealous, he was opening his arms and his heart to her. And she'll hurled it all back at him in a rage. But that rage had been building up in her for years. She saw that now. She'd done what she had to do, and when the evening lay in wreckage around them she'd stormed out of the house.

She'd wandered the moonlit grounds for an hour before returning quietly to the house. There was a light in a downstairs window, and she could see him there, watching the garden for her return. She approached the French doors, letting him see that she was safe, then hurried on upstairs to her room. He hadn't tried to come to her.

Now she slipped out of bed and went to the window, overlooking the pool. How inviting the water looked in the dazzling moonlight! How cool it would feel on her fevered skin!

She covered her nakedness with a terry cloth robe and crept quietly out into the corridor, pausing briefly outside the opposite door. Luke didn't snore, as he would have been the first to assert, but he had a muted rumble that she thought she could just discern. She opened the door a crack. He was growling in his sleep like a contented lion. Silently Pippa closed the door and slipped away down the stairs.

At the waterside she paused, looking up a moment at the blind windows of the house. There was nobody to see her daring. Still wearing the robe, she sat on the edge. At the last moment she tossed it away and slipped, naked, into the water. The sudden sense of freedom was wonderful. She turned over and over, relishing the coolness against her skin and the feeling of peace.

Luke sat up suddenly in bed. Far back in his consciousness he thought he'd heard a door close. He got up and went hopefully to the door, but there was nobody on the other side.

Well, what did you expect, you jerk? After the earful of home truths she gave you, you think she's going to come to your room? And she sure as hell doesn't want you going to hers.

He stood still, listening, but the only sound was the soft rustle of the net curtains at the tall windows,

lked off at once because I thought hanging
ound would have been pathetic.''

They looked at each other.

"We could have had it then,'' she whispered. ''If
I only stayed a little longer—if I hadn't put my
ide first, we could have been together all these
ears.'' She put her head in her hands and wept.

"My darling, don't.'' He got up onto the bed be-
de her and took her in his arms. "Don't, please
on't. It's no good looking back.''

"But the years we wasted. I can't bear it. All this
ime we could have been together.'' She clung to
him, sobbing in a kind of angry despair.

"Pippa—Pippa, please—look at me, darling—
don't cry—please don't cry.''

He could almost have wept himself. There was an
unfamiliar pain in his heart at the lost years, and her
pain made it greater. He kissed her tear-stained
cheeks, seeking to console her, for until she was
happy again he knew that nothing would go right
with him. Suddenly he was kissing her mouth, and
it was as warm and soft to him as it had been hard
and unwelcoming before.

Pippa reached for him eagerly. She was in Luke's
arms again, and this time it was right. The old magic
was working, flooding her senses with sweetness,
telling her she was where she belonged. He was hers
as she had always been his, and now she was free
to tell him so with her lips, her hands, her loins.

A slight tug and her robe fell open. She shrugged
it quickly aside, pulled at his towel and they were
naked together. He touched her reverently. He
seemed to have suffered a mysterious loss of con-
fidence. There was a hesitancy in his manner as

moving slightly in the breeze, and a soft splash from
the pool.

From the pool?

He parted the curtains of the hall window and
looked out in wonder at the scene below. A mermaid
was darting here and there in the water.

He was downstairs in a moment, a towel wrapped
around his middle. Pippa was gliding away from
him, oblivious. At the poolside he dropped the towel
by the diving board and went out to stand on the
edge. A slight creak of the board alerted her and she
rolled over on her back just in time to see Luke, as
naked as she, flying through the air. The gleaming
surface broke into a thousand fragments as he struck
the water and vanished.

She felt the disturbance as he neared her, and dog-
paddled, waiting for his head to break the surface,
then she turned and glided away. He came after her,
caught up, but didn't try to touch her, swimming
silently by her side.

Suddenly she dived. For a moment he had a rav-
ishing picture of a rounded, shimmering bottom
breaking the surface before vanishing. He dived with
her, and in the darkness below he touched her hand.
But he retreated at once, and when she came up she
couldn't find him at first.

He was at the far end, his back to her, and this
would have been a good chance to climb out and
return to bed. Instead she joined him in the deep
water and they swam silently, side by side. At this
moment she could hardly believe that she was ill.
She felt better and stronger than she'd done for ages.

At the pool's edge they turned together and, as if
by a signal, both changed to the backstroke, finding

in movement the harmony that had eluded them in words. In the shallow end they stood, and he took her hand, looking into her face. She looked back at him. They had come to the end of a confusing journey. What now?

His face was in shadow, but something told her that he was asking the same question, and everything depended on her answer. She let her head fall back so that her mouth was raised, close to his, expectant. Still holding her hand he leaned down and touched her lips with his own, as lightly as a feather. She swayed closer toward him, her thighs touching his, her breasts pressed against his chest. He put his arms around her, she wrapped hers around him, and they stood together for a long time, motionless, gleaming in the moonlight.

"Come back to me," he whispered. "Please come back to me."

This might have been the moment to apologize for her bitter words, but a wise instinct held her silent. It had all needed to be said, and perhaps, with that done, they could find a way forward. She said nothing, but rested her head on his shoulder.

"Come inside," he said. "You'll catch a cold out here."

Upstairs he fetched fresh towels from the bathroom, brought them to her room and settled on the floor, drying her feet. From this angle she couldn't see his face, and perhaps that was why he had chosen it.

"Do you want to leave?" he asked quietly.

"No."

"Are you sure? I'll drive you home, and I won't trouble you. I got it wrong. Everything you said is

true, but I thought I could make it rig was just my conceit."

"Luke, stop." She laid her fingers mouth. He took her hand, turned it an back with his lips.

"I'm sorry," he said. "I knew, really dream, but you didn't have the chance because I left you with all the burdens. when you said about always cooking realized what I'd done to you." He kiss again, and kept hold of it.

"Did you mean it?" he asked, in a "About wishing you'd never met me?"

"No, I didn't mean that."

"Of course not, because of Josie, but—

"Not just because of Josie. I wouldn' lose what we had. It was so beautiful."

"It was the most beautiful thing that pened to me. And when I found that I'd love with you again—or still loved you— both perhaps—I thought..." Luke made a frustration, "Dammit, I can find the wor enough when they don't mean anything." up. "But not with you."

She brushed the hair out of his eyes, down into his face with love.

"Was it true what you told me," sh "about turning back at the airport?"

"Yes. I couldn't believe that you'd reall go, but you did. So I turned back. It half ki to be the one to crack first, but you meant me than pride. And you weren't there."

"I was too proud to stay," she confes

though he were asking for reassurance every step of the way. She gave it to him joyfully. She, too, needed reassurance, and she found it in the love in his eyes and the gentleness of his touch.

Pippa had tried to imagine the woman she had become making love with the man he had become, but the vision always collapsed against the memory of their younger selves, feverish and frantic, thinking pleasure was everything. The pleasure was still there, but it had changed character. Once their matings had been fierce, volatile, but always with an underlying tenderness. Now the tenderness was greater, infusing every gesture and every whispered word.

"Tell me that you want me," he murmured. "I need to hear you say it."

"I never stopped wanting you."

"But now—this moment?"

"Now—and always."

As he entered her, Pippa felt a profound peace overtake her, as though all was now well because she had returned to where she was meant to be. And it was the most wonderful place on earth, a place where the storms were stilled and only joy remained. With his old instinctive understanding of her Luke made love with her now in just the way she needed, cradling her as though she was something precious and breakable that he feared to harm.

As they lay in each other's arms afterward he said, "There was never really anyone else. Only you." Certain memories assailed him and he added hastily, "However it may have looked."

Pippa smiled. "It's all right. I know what you mean." And she did.

It had never been like this before. Their young
selves had collapsed with exhaustion, not lain together in such deep, healing calm.

"I've been thinking," he murmured after a while.
"Perhaps it's as well that you left the barrier when
you did. We were kids. If we'd married then, we
might not have lasted. I wouldn't have left you, but
I'd have been lousy as a husband, and you'd have
gotten fed up and thrown me out. As it is, we've got
years and years ahead of us."

"Years and years," she echoed wistfully. "Oh,
Luke, I do hope so."

"Of course we have. We'll see our golden wedding, and I'll look back and remind you of tonight."
He grinned. "Josie will be sixty by then, fussing
around her grandchildren. Can you imagine that?
And I'll be in my eighties, still relying on you to
keep me on the straight and narrow. As long as I
have you I'll be all right. But—" his arms tightened
suddenly, and for the first time ever she heard a note
of fear in his voice "—but you have to be there. I
faced life without you once before, but I couldn't
face it again."

"Hush," she whispered, "don't say things like
that."

"I know I'm talking nonsense. It's just that I can't
believe how lucky I am to have been given a second
chance."

For a while he went on talking in a soft murmur.
The future entranced him, and he dwelt on it lovingly as the minutes drifted away and she nestled
against the warmth of his body. Then something
struck him.

"Hey, I've just remembered what I was going to

ask you. When you were mad at me you said—what was it? Oh, yes, 'when it's almost too late for me.' What did you mean by that? Darling? Pippa?''

But she was asleep.

Cinderella's ball lasted for three beautiful days. One perfect moment followed another in such profusion that they both lost the sense of time, and everything seemed to be happening at once.

They talked endlessly, as though no barriers had ever existed between them. Pippa found the photographs she'd brought with her, meaning to show them all to him.

''Things started happening so fast that it kept going out of my head, but I would like you to see them. I'm a compulsive picture taker, and they'll fill in so many gaps for you. She was one day old here.''

He looked slowly through the pictures. Long ago Pippa had sent him one from this set, and so he'd thought he knew what his newborn daughter looked like. Now he saw that one picture could only convey a fraction of the truth. Here were a dozen tiny Josies, mostly asleep, but one with her eyes barely open, looking bruised and battered from her perilous voyage. Something caught at his throat as he realized that he hadn't been there to greet her.

But so many other people had been there, he realized jealously. There was Angus and Michael, Liz, Sarah—all the old gang who'd lived at the guest house in those days, crowded around the bed, raising champagne glasses, while Pippa held her little bundle shoulder high for the camera.

But not him.

Here was another close-up of Josie, tiny fists raised high to tell the world that she'd arrived now, and it had better watch out. And Pippa again, also looking bruised and battered, her face full of a touching mixture of triumph and vulnerability.

In all the years apart he'd been thinking of her as the same Pippa, growing a little older perhaps, but the same. Now he saw that the minute scrap in her arms had taken her on to a new stage of life. One where he hadn't followed.

More pictures. There was his little girl in a pink party dress, facing a cake, trying to blow out three candles.

"Her third birthday," he murmured.

"That huge giraffe beside her was your present."

"My—"

"You sent some money and I bought it. It was her favorite. She went around telling everyone that Daddy gave it to her."

"Pippa—don't." He closed his eyes.

"Darling, I wasn't thinking. I didn't mean to rub it in."

"I know you didn't. It's just that it's all gone, forever. And I didn't realize."

There were more birthday pics, third, fourth, fifth, and now Josie was showing the first signs of the child she was today, the face growing finer, the eyes already hinting at a cool intelligence working away behind the childish features.

"She learned to talk early," Pippa recalled, "and boy did she talk! She was the first in her class to learn to read and she never stopped asking questions. She went around interrogating everyone at the guest house. I told them not to let her pester, but none of them shooed her away.''

He thought of being ''pestered'' by a bright-eyed little girl who wanted his company more than anything. Like that kiddy in the park in London, long ago, crying, ''Daddy, Daddy, come here, I want you.'' And her jerk of a father had got mad at her, instead of understanding that he was privileged. But at least he'd stayed with her. Not like another jerk.

Pippa didn't seem to have noticed his reverie.

''Josie's like a sponge,'' she was saying, ''she just sops up knowledge and experience and never forgets. Her teachers think she might be something really brilliant in computers.''

''Not the greatest cook in the world?'' he asked, dismayed.

''Only in her spare time.'' She laughed. ''Look at this one.''

It showed Josie in a blue frock, her head covered in a tea towel held down by a circle of tinsel, clutching a cushion wrapped in a shawl. Beside her stood a scowling little boy, also equipped with tea towel and tinsel halo.

''That's her being Mary in the school Nativity play. She was seven. The cushion is meant to be the baby. But don't be fooled by that saintly look. Two minutes after this was taken she had a bust-up with Joseph. He knocked her halo off, and she walloped him with the cushion.''

Luke shouted with laughter. ''There's a chip off the old block!''

''Whose old block?''

''Yours, mine, her great aunt Clarrie maybe. She comes from the same kind of stock on both sides, folk who like to make a nuisance of themselves. Have you got any more?''

''This one was last year, and the Labrador with her is George. He belonged to a lady called Helen, a financial genius who'd stayed with us years earlier. Josie loved her because she could play with George, who was a puppy, and I liked her because she rearranged all my financial affairs so that I was more profitable. Then one day the police called, and the next thing we knew Helen had dumped George in Josie's arms and vanished out of a back window. She was wanted for fraud, but they never caught her. She sends us a postcard from the Bahamas every Christmas.

''George turned out to be valuable, and as Helen had left his papers we were able to use him for stud, and did very well out of him.'' Pippa laughed. ''That was how Josie learned about sex. She became his 'manager.' He died last year in a car accident. She cried for a month.''

In whose arms? Not his, that was for sure!

They called Josie constantly but were lucky to speak to her. These days all her time was spent at the zoo, where she'd fallen in love with Billy and Tara and Ruby and Gita, all elephants. When they did find her in, she would talk about her new friends as though they were people. It was clear she was having a wonderful time.

''I guess I've just discovered another aspect of being a parent,'' Luke said ruefully. ''It's calling to say, 'How are you, darling? I miss my little girl.' and getting, 'Daddy, guess what Billy did today!' I've been jilted before, but never for a elephant.''

Pippa chuckled. ''You're learning.''

They were together every moment, except once when Luke left her behind while he vanished for an hour, only to be mysterious on his return. They would talk about driving into town to eat out, but always settle for a candlelit table just inside the French doors overlooking the pool. Afterward they would stretch out on one of the huge sofas, idly zapping television channels, too lost in each other to take notice of the screen, until Pippa usually fell asleep in his arms.

One night he said, "It's not too late, is it? We can still have it all."

"Nobody gets it all. We've got now, and it's far more than I ever thought we'd have."

"Say you'll marry me," he pleaded.

"I want to marry you. Oh, Luke, if you only knew how much I want that."

"That's good enough for me. Here." He reached under the cushion and brought out a small box. "This is what I went to buy this morning."

Inside the box was a ring, set with one large, perfect diamond, and surrounded by a cluster of small ones. She gasped at its perfection.

"I'll change it if you don't like it, but I thought this suited you."

"Luke, I—"

"Please put it on, my love. And keep it. And say that we'll add another one to it, very soon."

She slipped it on. It was a beautiful ring, and she kissed it lovingly. He didn't seem to notice that she hadn't said what he wanted.

The days became one long perfect day, until at last it was time to go. The last swim, the last of

Sonia's wonderful meals, the goodbyes to the servants, who'd been observing everything, doing their bit to help the romance along and then fading into the background, but never so far that they couldn't watch with delight.

Luke found Pippa sitting by the pool, staring into the water, her eyes fixed on something deep inside her. "Are you ready to go?" he asked gently.

She shook her head. "I shall never be ready to leave here," she said wistfully. "We were so happy."

"Because we found each other."

"Yes, and because we managed to shut the world out. It's as unreal here as Disneyland. When we leave—"

"It won't vanish. We have our own reality, and it'll come with us. We don't need places, just us. From now on we'll always be happy."

"Always," she whispered. "I wonder what *always* will mean for us."

"It means growing old and gray together, and loving each other through everything that happens."

"And forgiving each other?"

"If that means you've forgiven me, then yes. But you could never do anything I needed to forgive. I know that everything about you is good and true."

"Luke, there's something I—"

"Hush," he said, kissing her. "What do we need to say? I love you. I will always love you, until the end of time. Tell me that you feel the same."

"You know I do."

"I want to hear you say it. I want you to say it often, for all the times you might have said it in the past and didn't because you knew I wasn't ready to hear. Say it, my darling.''

''I love you, Luke—''

''Until the end of time?''

''Yes,'' she said huskily. ''Until the end of time—whenever that is.''

He brushed a stray lock of hair back with tender fingers. ''What a strange thing to say. Time will never end, just as we will never end.''

Suddenly she was clinging to him. ''Oh, Luke— Luke—''

''Darling, what is it?''

''Hold me. Don't let me go.''

She wanted to cry out, ''Don't let me go into that dark place that might take me away from you. I'm not ready—''

''I'll never let you go,'' he promised.

She searched his face. ''Luke, you really do love me, don't you? You'll love me whatever happens?''

''Nothing could happen to make me stop loving you. Nothing at all.''

They drove back to Manhattan Beach in the late afternoon. At Pippa's suggestion they left collecting Josie until the following morning. She planned to use this final evening to explain things to Luke. All the way home she was working out how to tell him gently that in a few days she must have an operation that would either save her or not. And if not—she wouldn't think about that. They would come through this and have a future together. For a moment the wall of black ice was there again, barring her path. She covered her eyes with her hand, refusing to see it. In her newfound love and strength she would not admit that it could all be taken away.

The sun was setting as they reached home. "Just time for a dip in the sea," Luke said.

"All right." She would tell him over supper.

Just as everything had been silver the night they'd swum in the pool, now everything was deep gold. The beach was emptying fast, the tide was out, and if they turned their backs to the land there was only the empty sea and the sky.

"It's like having the world to ourselves," Luke said.

"If we could only keep it like this." She sighed. "With just Josie. Nobody else."

"We will. We'll create our own place. We're lucky. I'll make it up to you, Pippa. You'll be the happiest woman alive. What is it?"

"Nothing," she said quickly.

"You flinched. What did I say?"

"You imagined it. Let's go back."

They began to walk slowly up the beach, hand in hand. At the last moment he stopped and turned, his arms around her waist, leaning back to look at her, golden in the light of the setting sun.

"You're beautiful," he said. "You've always been beautiful, but never so much as at this moment, my love."

"My love," she echoed softly. "My love, oh, my love."

"My love, as you've always been." He drew her against him.

"Darling, people will see."

"Let them. Everyone's crazy on this beach, anyway. Kiss me, Pippa. We have so much to make up for."

Keeping his mouth on hers he took her hand and

began to tread carefully up the rest of the beach.
The few drifters who were out at that time of the
evening parted, laughing, to let them pass. The sun
was growing richer in color as it dipped to the ho-
rizon, and for a moment it seemed as though the
whole world wanted to stop and gaze on this golden
couple who walked in a golden light to a golden
future. Whatever the secret was, it seemed as though
they had cracked it.

Across the Strand, then up the walk to the doorway, still with his lips on hers, his body warm
against her skin.

"Quickly," he murmured. "Let's get inside so
that I can have my wicked way with you."

"Mmm!"

Entranced by him, she failed to notice the two
figures standing by Luke's door. And she was almost on top of them before she realized that it was
Frank and Elly, their faces set in masks of frozen
disapproval.

Chapter Eleven

"Frank, Elly," Pippa whispered the words, "how...how lovely to see you."

"We were worried about you," Elly said, putting her arms around Pippa. "Darling, we have to talk—"

"Later," Pippa said quickly. "Let's get inside first."

Luke opened the door, and when they were all inside he turned to Frank and Elly, smiling. It wasn't the moment he would have chosen to be interrupted, and they weren't his favorite people, but he was, as he said afterward in some bitterness, happy enough to greet the devil himself.

"We met before," he said, taking Frank's unresponsive hand. "I was at your wedding. Elly—" he embraced her "—good to see you looking so well."

"We're all well," Pippa said quickly. "I've never

felt better in my life. Now admit it, you two. Aren't I a big improvement on that pallid creature who left London?'' She was talking too fast and in an unnatural voice, but she had to warn them off the dangerous subject.

''You've got a good color,'' Frank conceded grudgingly.

''Good color!'' Luke exclaimed indignantly. ''She looks great.'' He planted another quick kiss on her cheek. ''Honey, put some coffee on while I—while I put *something* on.'' He vanished hastily.

''Darling, are you mad?'' Elly asked as soon as he'd gone. ''Staying here when your operation—''

''I'll be home for that. It's not until the end of this week.''

''You should be resting to be ready for it,'' Frank almost shouted.

''Frank—please—you know why I came.''

''Yes, I do,'' he said bitterly, ''some foolishness about Josie meeting her father—who's taken no interest in her since she was born.''

''That's not true. He's supported her.''

''But he's never bothered to meet her, or you wouldn't have needed to take this crazy trip, risking your life—''

''What was that?''

They all turned to see Luke standing in the door. He was wearing jeans, but his chest was still bare, and it was rising and falling as though he'd just received a shock and was finding it hard to breathe.

Oh, God! Pippa thought. Not like this. I never meant him to find out like this.

''What did you say?'' he asked Frank. His face was very pale.

"I said that Pippa is a very sick woman, was probably dying—before she ever came here—"

"That's not true," Pippa said quickly. "The doctor said I had a good chance—"

"He said you had a fair-to-middling chance if you had the operation quickly and didn't do anything stupid," Frank growled. "He didn't reckon on you taking a long flight over the Atlantic and another one back. Do you know how dangerous that is? As for what's gone on since you've been here—can you honestly say you've taken care?"

She barely heard him. Her eyes were on Luke's face as he turned to her. He looked puzzled, as though he heard the words but could put no meaning to them.

"Pippa?" he said quietly. "What is this crazy man talking about?"

"Frank isn't crazy, Luke. He's just blown things up out of all proportion. I've been a bit poorly recently—"

"Yes, you told me, asthma—"

"Asthma be blowed!" Frank exploded. "She's got mitral stenosis. You know what that is, do you, Danton? It's a malfunction of the mitral valve of the heart. It's a killer. It killed her mother. It's killing her."

Luke might not have heard him for all the notice he took. His eyes, full of a dreadful question, were still fixed on Pippa's face.

"Yes," she said despairingly. "It's true."

"But...I don't understand. You can't be ill. I've seen you every day, and you've been fine."

"You mean she's fooled you into thinking she's fine," Frank said with a sneer. "I don't suppose it's hard to fool you where your own convenience is concerned.''

''Please, Frank,'' Pippa whispered. ''This isn't the way.''

''And what is the way? Making it easy for him the way you've always done? All these years you've let him be a father on easy terms because those are the only terms he's interested in.''

''Frank, hush!'' Elly protested. ''Josie may be about somewhere.''

''No, she's with my parents,'' Luke said.

''How convenient,'' Frank said disparagingly. ''A real takeover bid—now that it suits you.''

''What do you mean by that?'' Luke demanded.

''I mean I've seen the Web site. Making use of your own child to make yourself look good. How could you let him do it?'' He turned on Pippa.

''Josie wanted it, Frank. It made her happy.''

''You don't give a child something that's bad for her just because she wants it. She needs adults who'll protect her, not exploit her for their own cheap ends.''

''If it wasn't for Pippa I'd knock you down for saying that,'' Luke said in a harsh voice. ''I love my daughter.''

''Your daughter,'' Frank sneered. ''That's rich, coming from you. What kind of father have you been? Sure, you've supported her, but money's easy. When did you do anything that wasn't easy?''

''I'm not arguing with you. I've told you, I love my daughter, and I love Pippa. We're going to be married. The past is the past. If Pippa and Josie can forgive me for it, then it's nobody else's damned business. Including yours.''

Frank completely lost control. "You fool!" he screamed. "Don't you understand, *she's dying!* If you'd treated her properly all those years ago she wouldn't have had to take this insane risk to find you now."

"Frank—" Pippa and Elly both tried to silence him together, but he was like a man possessed.

"That operation is her last chance," he screamed, "and it's a very small one. What are you going to do when she's dead, eh? What's all your fine talk going to be worth *when she's dead?*"

Watching Luke, Pippa realized that until that moment he hadn't fully taken it in. He didn't speak, but his face seemed to grow withered before her eyes. Her head was beginning to swim. "Frank, that's enough. I think you should go now."

"I'll go when you come with me."

"I'll come when I'm ready. Please, Frank, you shouldn't have done this. Just tell me where I can find you."

"At the airport hotel," Elly said.

But Frank wasn't about to give up. "I still think we should wait and—"

"Go!" Pippa said with soft vehemence.

Elly drew him away, leaving Pippa and Luke alone together. She could hardly bear to look at him. He was breathing hard like a man who'd been punched over the heart.

"Dear God!" he said softly.

"I was going to tell you tonight."

"Or tomorrow? Or the next day?"

"Yes, I've been putting it off. But it would have been tonight, because I have to go home. Oh, Luke,

I'm so sorry you found out this way. It wasn't meant to happen.''

She touched him. He was trembling.

"I can't take this in," he said at last. "How long have you known?"

"A few weeks. I didn't know what to do. Suddenly there were so many things to be thought of, all at once."

"You could have picked up the phone and called me then. I could have come over to England—"

"Would you have?" she asked wistfully.

"Of course I would. There was no need for this. I'd have come at once. I might have been able to help you cope with all those things you mentioned." He looked at her distantly. "But you never even thought of turning to me, did you?"

"No, I didn't," she admitted.

"Well, I guess I only have myself to blame for that," he said in deep bitterness. "You don't have to say it."

"I wasn't going to."

There were tears in his eyes. He thumped his fist on the breakfast bar, then pulled her into his arms and held her fiercely. "Dear God!" he wept. "Pippa, *Pippa!*"

"It's going to be all right," she said, clasping him. "It has to be. We can't lose each other now."

"Can't we?" he asked hoarsely. "Frank seemed very sure."

"Frank's an old woman, he's panicking."

They clung to each other. Pippa was remembering the fear and shock that came with the first discovery. She'd faced it long ago, and from the reserves of strength she'd built up since, she could help him now.

But she'd forgotten the anger. In the first few hours of knowing she might die, she'd been swept by a terrible rage. It was different from the lively, combative spirit with which she'd always faced the world. That had been a searing, blistering fury against whatever had done this to her and to Josie, the little girl who might lose her mother. She had wanted to scream and scream at an unjust fate.

But that wasn't in her mind now, and when she felt Luke shaking violently in her arms, she didn't at first realize that he, too, had been swept by devastating anger. So his next remark came as a shock.

"But at least you told Frank the truth, which is a damned sight more than you did with me."

"I couldn't help that. It was forced on me by circumstances."

"But all this time you've had a secret agenda, haven't you? I thought we were close again, but how close could we be when you were hiding such a secret? Why did you really turn up here suddenly?"

"Because I knew I might not have very long, and I wanted to make sure you met Josie while there was time. All these years—I thought you might have come to see her just once. But you never did, and if…if Frank and Elly have to become her parents— they're good people—kind and reliable, and she'll need that. But I wanted her to know you, too. I wanted you to meet her and love her so that you'd never want to lose touch with her."

He released her and drew back, looked at her strangely, as though trying to work out who she was.

"Luke," she cried, "please try to understand. I did what I had to."

"Yeah, I get that."

"Then what? What is it you blame me for?"

"Deceiving me," he said quietly. "Letting me live in a fool's paradise." He gave a mirthless laugh. "The operative word being *fool*. All this time—telling myself fairy tales about a second chance—you should have been honest with me."

"When? And how? The day I arrived, maybe? When I walked through that door and you threw your arms around me because I was your escape route from Dominique. I knew then that you were the same man I'd known, only it was a bit weird because eleven years had passed and you *shouldn't* have been the same."

"And afterward? You knew I was falling in love with you. I was making plans for our future, and you let me make them although you knew there might not be a future—dear God!"

Her temper flared. She faced him squarely, and there was a steely look in her eyes that was new to him.

"And just what should I have told you, Luke? That I might be dying so that you could be careful not to love me? I should have warned you to hold off and not let your feelings get too deep in case you got hurt? You're very good at holding off, aren't you? Good at protecting yourself by not getting too involved. That's how you survive. By never getting too close to anyone. Generous, great-hearted Luke, with a smile for everyone and a heart for nobody."

"That's not what I meant," he cried angrily.

"I think it is. You'd have liked to know, so that you could give just so much and no more."

He paled with shock. "I don't believe you said that to me," he whispered.

"Why not? It's how it's always been with you. Over the years I've gotten used to it. Only I'd forgotten—since I came here, I'd forgotten—and that was very silly of me—"

Appalled, they stared at each other and at the abyss that yawned between them. They no longer looked the same to each other. He saw a woman who'd snubbed him to take the hardest journey alone, who'd spoken of love while secretly despising him. She saw a man who'd fooled her with pretty promises it wasn't in him to keep. Luke's promises were always pretty, she thought in anguish. Best hung on the wall to be admired, but not for everyday use.

She wanted to tell him that she hadn't meant the last words. They were needlessly cruel because she was angry and bitter. But the seconds passed and she couldn't speak.

"I think I'll go out for a while," he said after a moment. "I need to do some thinking."

"Sure," she said listlessly. She didn't look up when the door closed, and the next moment she heard his car drive away.

Luke had meant to be away for an hour at most, but once on the freeway he seemed to go into a hypnotic trance in which there was nothing but a stream of traffic coming from infinity and going to infinity. He was cold with shock, terrified, disorientated, an alien in a strange universe.

All the familiar places had vanished, or tilted into ugly, unrecognizable shapes that taunted him with his own uselessness. Somehow the earth had turned back on its axis, and his life seemed to be whirling past him in reverse order. It was yesterday and he was completely happy with the woman he loved, their hearts and minds open to each other—except that hers wasn't open to him at all.

It was last week, and she was walking through his door with Josie, transforming a life that had been growing increasingly empty and pointless. He wanted to reach out and seize that moment, because if he could do that everything might still come right. But it was whisked out of his hand and away into the darkness, and suddenly he was back eleven years, saying goodbye at the airport, leaving her, knowing it was all wrong. And that was the moment where he really wanted to stop the world. And it was too late.

He lost track of time. The darkness turned into dawn and still he drove. He stopped for gas and returned to the car like a zombie. When he finally halted at a motel he had to detach his hands from the steering wheel one finger at a time.

He checked in and called home, but there was no answer. She must be asleep. He called his parents, who said Pippa and Claudia had collected Josie hours earlier. She'd seemed cheerful and normal, and somehow that made his heart sink because it reminded him how hard it was to know what Pippa was really thinking. But then he recalled that Claudia had been with her, and he felt better.

He tried calling her again and again, but there was never a reply, and at last he fell asleep with his hand on the phone. At first light he started the long journey back, driving as fast as he dared.

He told himself that now he'd got everything under control. There was no way he would let her fly back to England. She must stay here, and he'd book her into the finest hospital with the finest surgeons. He would get her the best of everything, and when she left the hospital he would wait on her hand and foot, caring for her as no woman had ever been cared for before. She would get well, and their future would go on as before. He tried to shut out the sound of the phone ringing and ringing without answer.

It was late afternoon when he reached his house. Even before he opened the back door he could see a shadow inside, and relief swept over him. *"Pippa!"*

But it wasn't Pippa.

"She's gone, Luke," Claudia said. "She flew back to England yesterday. I got here just as she was leaving. She told me what had happened."

"And you let her go?"

"I couldn't stop her. It's her decision, and by all accounts she shouldn't put that operation off too long. Why should I try to make her stay? So that you could quarrel with her again? Do you think she could take that?"

"How much did she tell you?"

"Everything. I knew she wasn't well. I gave her the name of my doctor in Montecito—"

"You knew she was ill?"

"So would you have, if you'd used your eyes. Those headaches that kept happening, the shortness of breath—yes, I know she had an explanation, but

it was all too much, and it happened too often for a
young woman. I don't think she really had headaches at all. They were an excuse to lie down and
save her energy.''

''Why didn't you say this before?''

''It wasn't for me to tell you. She had the right
to pick her own time. Besides, I didn't guess how
seriously ill she was. When you think what she's
gone through, keeping it to herself, nobody to con-
fide in. And always looking at the future, wondering
if it's a blank, and smiling, pretending. It must have
been so lonely. I don't know how she endured it.
Oh, Luke, sweetie—'' He was weeping.

''Years ago, we used to tell each other everything,'' he said hoarsely.

''I doubt that. You might think it, but I'll bet there
was a lot she couldn't tell you because you didn't
want to know. Like how much she loved you.''

''Of course I wanted to know—''

''Now perhaps, but then? In those days, did you
ever tell her that you loved her?''

He fought to remember. ''Yes—no—I must
have—''

''I wonder. Love means chains to you, Luke. I
know that's true now, so I can imagine what you
were like then.''

He sat at the breakfast bar and rested his head on
his hands. ''What really hurts is that she shut me
out. All the time letting me think things were fine
when she was actually carrying that burden and not
letting me share it. Keeping me on the outside. I'd
have liked to help her, be there for her when she
was feeling bad. But obviously she doesn't think I

could do that. I'm fine for a holiday romance, but not for when things get serious, right?''

"I don't know," Claudia said. "Only Pippa could say."

"I tried to tell her this, but she just thought I was mad at her for not warning me, so that I could stop myself loving her. As though there was any way I could stop that. She actually said that I would have liked to have kept my distance—protected myself—"

"And wouldn't you?"

"No. I love Pippa. I always have. I pretended I didn't—who did I think I was fooling?"

"I think you fooled her," Claudia said.

Before her eyes his face changed, becoming older. "It's my own fault, isn't it?" he said slowly. "I made her think the worst of me. Why should she think anything else? I even ran away now. I didn't mean to. I wanted to come back quickly, but I lost track of time, and now she's gone." He closed his eyes. "Tell me some more about when you got here. What happened?"

"I drove her over to your parents to collect Josie, and then to the airport. Frank and Elly were there, and they all caught the night flight to London. Then I came back here to wait for you."

"I called," he said, wishing his brain wasn't so fuzzy. "There was no answer."

"I was probably still out seeing them off."

"Josie must have wondered why I wasn't there to say goodbye, poor little kid. Does she know how ill her mother is?"

"No. Pippa couldn't risk telling her before she told you, in case she let it out. Besides, I don't think she wanted anything to spoil Josie's time here. I did suggest that she should delay leaving because I didn't like the way she looked. I don't think the flight will be good for her. But she was adamant she wanted to get away.''

"Away from me," he said bitterly. "I thought I had a chance to put things right.''

Claudia's face was sympathetic, but her words were firm. "Luke, face it. You thought you could put things right for yourself. But you've got to put them right for her.''

"I've been a total jerk, haven't I?"

"Yes," Claudia said simply. "But at least you have the grace to see that you're a jerk. Which means that you're a redeemable jerk.''

"Thanks for that small comfort," he said wryly. "I think I'll have a shower.''

The shower cleared his brain slightly, but a clear view of things didn't make them look any better. He went to his bedroom to find clean clothes, and stopped at what he saw on the pillow. It was an envelope bearing his name in Pippa's unmistakable handwriting.

He'd never been a coward before but he found he was one now. He would do anything rather than read that letter with its message of finality. He would find her first, explain, ask her forgiveness. Then he would read the letter.

Even as these wild thoughts rushed through his brain he was opening the envelope with shaking hands. Pippa had written:

My darling Luke,
You were right, I should have told you from

the start. I always knew it. But, you see, I didn't
expect anything that happened. I thought it was
all over between us, certainly on your side. I
never thought you could love me again, but you
did, and I suppose I played you a shabby trick
in letting you plan for a future that I knew
might never happen. I kept meaning to tell you
and putting it off. Try to forgive me.

My main concern has always been Josie. She
loves you, and I want you to be part of her life,
whether I'm there or not. I've named Frank as
her guardian, but you can see plenty of her. I
shall make him promise that, and he's a man
of his word.

But please, please Luke, if it comes to the
worst, don't fight over her. Josie loves you, but
she loves Frank and Elly, too, and if you fight
it will make her unhappy. Poor little thing,
she'll have enough to cope with.

Goodbye, my dearest. Thank you for the
gifts you gave me. Josie first, but oh, so many
other wonderful things. If we don't see each
other again, don't remember the unkind things
I said to you. I didn't mean them. I've always
loved you for what you were, and not a different kind of man that you might have been. And
I always will.
Pippa.

There was something small and hard in the envelope. He tipped it out and found himself holding
the diamond ring he'd given her at Montecito, long
ago, in another life.

He sat and stared at the letter and the ring, feeling

his whole body grow cold with fear, until he was so paralyzed that he thought he might never move again.

When he finally managed it he reached stiffly for the phone and called the guest house in London. But the phone was answered by a grumpy new resident who knew nothing except that nobody was where they should be. He hung up, still dazed, and when Claudia brought him some more coffee he drank it mechanically.

"You'd better try to get some sleep," Claudia said.

"No, I'm getting the next flight to England."

"I've already booked you on the eight o'clock flight this evening. That's the first that had a seat free. Go to bed and I'll wake you in time."

"You're the best friend a man ever had."

She delivered him to LAX that night, and he caught the 8 p.m. flight to London Heathrow. It lasted eleven hours and he was awake for every moment, looking out of the tiny window at the darkness, with his mind playing tricks, for she seemed to be there.

Sometimes she was as he'd first seen her at eighteen in her outrageous clothes and the attitude to match. But then he saw her as she'd been in the past few days, apparently happy but concealing her secret, because he wasn't man enough to share it. Often she would be wearing the glorious silk robe Claudia had given her, and that would hurt him. "You should have only the best," he'd said, but he hadn't given her the best. By now she ought to have a wardrobe full of silk, given by the man who loved her.

He wished he could escape the night that offered such unbearable visions, and eventually he was lucky. Because London was eight hours ahead of Los Angeles, he was flying forward in time, and after barely a couple of hours of darkness, he saw the first glint of dawn.

But this was almost worse, because he began to reread her letter, and phrases stood out with new and hideous meanings.

"I've always loved you for what you were, and not a different kind of man that you might have been."

She had always known that he would let her down, and accepted it, and forgiven him. That was what she meant. She'd loved him as a woman loves a child, making allowances, asking nothing. And that, when you came right down to it, was the kind of love he'd always preferred. He put the letter away quickly, wondering if the flight would never end.

At last they landed. It was early afternoon, although his inner clock said dawn. With only one piece of hand luggage he got through the lines quickly. Heathrow had changed since he'd left it eleven years earlier, yet not so much that he couldn't identify the spot where he'd held Pippa for the last time. She'd smiled and teased him about flirting with some beauty on the flight, and he'd thought she didn't care. Now he wondered how he could have been so blind.

Blind and stupid! Blind and stupid!

And there was what looked like the very place where he'd retraced his steps to the gate, hoping to find her there still, and been so desolate that she was gone. And, fool that he was, he'd shrugged his hurt aside and said if that was how she felt, who needed her? And all the time he *had* needed her, but been too proud to say so, and now it might be too late.

He changed some money and found a taxi, thrusting several large bills into the hands of the startled driver and telling him to "Move it!" Even so it seemed to take eons to cover the twenty miles to London, and then a few more while they crawled through traffic jams to the center. But at last he was turning the old familiar corner, stopping outside the guest house.

The place looked different, he thought, pushing open the glass door. Smartened up out of all recognition. A stocky young woman in jeans came down the stairs, smiling a welcome.

"Pippa," he said tensely. "Where is she?"

"In hospital," the young woman said. "She flew back from America yesterday and they took her straight there. She was in a bad way."

A cold hand clutched him. "Her operation? She's had it?"

"No, they had to stabilize her first. They were hoping to do it this afternoon, I think."

"Where?"

"The Matthews Infirmary. It's—"

"I know it, thanks." It was where all the medical students came from. Luke was out of the door and running. There might still be time to see her first. There *had* to be. Because if not—

Because if not, she might die without ever knowing how much he loved her. And for that he would never forgive himself as long as he lived.

Chapter Twelve

At the infirmary he gave Pippa's name to the receptionist.

"On the eighth floor," she said. "But I'm telling you what I've told all the others. You can't go in, and it's going to be a long wait."

"All the others?"

"Ms. Davis seems to have a lot of friends."

The ride up was long enough for him to realize he was walking into the unknown. Josie had known nothing, but she would have been told by now, and some of it would have come from Frank. He wondered if his daughter hated him. For himself, he could bear that burden, as deserved. But when he thought of what it would do to her, the world seemed to grow dark.

As soon as he stepped out of the lift he saw what the receptionist had meant. A crowd had gathered in the corridor. Luke counted seven before he identified Frank, Elly and—

"Josie!"

"Daddy!" The little girl's shriek split the air, and the next moment she'd evaded Frank's detaining hand to dash down the corridor straight into Luke's waiting arms.

"I knew you'd come," she said frantically. "Uncle Frank said you wouldn't. He said you were horrid to Mommy and you'd helped make her sick and you'd never really loved her and—"

Luke's eyes met Frank's over Josie's head. "You've been saying a lot of things, Frank," he said coldly. "Most of them you had no right to say."

"And you have no right to be here," Frank said in a tight voice. "How dare you come barging in, upsetting the child—"

"I reckon she'd be a sight more upset if I hadn't come."

"You're nothing here. If Pippa had wanted you, she'd have stayed with you."

"We'll talk about this some other time," Luke said, giving him a warning glance. "For the moment I'd like to know how she is."

Elly had come to join them. "They're operating. It's been a long job, but they should be through quite soon."

The others drifted across and introduced themselves. They were the current crop of house guests. Luke picked up Harry, Jake, Davina, and his mind refused to take in any more. They regarded him without condemnation, but with a lot of curiosity.

Josie kept a tight hold on Luke's hand to make

him sit beside her. "Daddy, why did Mommy leave like that? *Were* you horrid to her?"

"Tell her everything, if you dare," Frank jeered.

"All right, I will. Yes, darling, Mommy and I did have a quarrel, and it was my fault." A tremor shook him. "All my fault. I came to tell her I'm sorry."

"But why? What did you do?"

"When I found out that she was ill, I didn't understand why she hadn't confided in me. I blamed her."

Josie's eyes filled with tears. "Me, too. Oh Daddy, I got mad at her on the plane. I didn't mean to but I couldn't help it. And when we landed she collapsed, and it's all my fault—" She burst into sobs.

Luke gathered her into his arms. "It's not your fault, darling. It's mine if anyone's. She should have told both of us, but you see, Mommy's a very strong person. She tends to shoulder all the burdens herself, so that other people can be happy—" his voice wavered "—and then you find out that she's been bearing things alone, and you feel kind of hurt that she didn't share it with you. But you have to understand—you have to understand—that she doesn't mean…" His voice ran down. He tried to hide his despair from the child, but he couldn't do it, and his head sank until it was resting against hers.

They didn't move after that. Nor did anyone else go near the man and the child, enclosed in their own world, needing only each other.

Nobody knew how many hours passed before there was a noise at the end of the corridor as the doors were opened so that a bed could be wheeled through. It was accompanied by a doctor and two nurses, one of whom was holding a drip that was connected to the woman lying on the bed. Everybody stood up tensely to watch the little procession approach and turn into the room opposite. Luke caught the barest glimpse of Pippa's face as she passed, and felt his daughter's hand seek his.

The doctor faced them. "She's not as strong as I'd like, but she's holding on. The next few hours will be vital."

"But she's going to live?" came Frank's voice. "Surely you can say that much?"

The doctor hesitated. "It's too soon to make any promises."

"I want to see Mommy," Josie said.

"In a few minutes," the doctor said, "when they've finished settling her. Just you and one other person—perhaps the next of kin—"

"I'm her next of kin," Frank said through gritted teeth, "since she isn't married."

Luke flinched, but he didn't retaliate, because into his head had come the memory of Pippa's words in the letter. *If you fight with Frank it will make her unhappy...*

"Daddy—" Josie reached for him, but he forced himself to step back.

"I'll wait," he said.

"No," Elly said, intervening. "You're the one she wants." She laid a gentle hand on her husband's arm, silencing his protest.

Hand in hand, father and daughter slipped into Pippa's room, and Luke couldn't have said which of them was clinging to the other more desperately for comfort. The sight of Pippa horrified him. She lay as still as death, her eyes closed, her face the color of parchment. On each side she was attached to drips or machinery that seemed to overwhelm her. Like any creature that lived mainly through its senses Luke recoiled from illness. But now all he could think of was how small and frail she looked and how he would have liked to gather her protectively in his arms. But he couldn't.

"Can we touch her?" he asked at last.

"Better not," advised one of the nurses.

"What are her chances?"

"Her color's reasonably good, and she's stable. That's really all we can say for the moment. I think you should go now."

Outside in the corridor Luke repeated the nurse's words to everyone, but speaking mainly to Frank, keeping his voice gentle, trying not to react to the open dislike on the other man's face.

Everyone settled down for a long wait. Somebody went for coffee and sandwiches. A silence fell. The clock ticked on as the light faded into darkness. Josie was allowed back in to see her mother.

"Daddy—"

"Take your uncle Frank, honey," he said. "He loves her, too."

He had to force the words out. Only the conviction that he was doing what Pippa would have wanted made it possible. Frank regarded him with suspicion and went on into the room.

"That was very nice of you," Elly said when Frank and Josie had gone.

"It's Pippa, she—" He couldn't say any more, but he suddenly noticed how kind Elly's eyes were. He wondered why he'd never seen it before, and felt ashamed that he'd ever seen her as a person to make fun of. On impulse he pulled Pippa's letter out. "She wouldn't mind my showing you this."

He pointed to the end of the letter where Pippa had written, "Josie loves you, but she loves Frank and Elly, too, and if you fight it will make her unhappy."

"Thank you," she said, giving it back to him. "I'll try to make Frank understand."

Josie slipped out and came to Luke. "She's just the same," she said.

"No sign of waking up?"

"No, they say she won't tonight, because she's being kept under heavy sedation. They'll start lifting it tomorrow."

"They say we might as well go home for the night," Frank said.

"That's a good idea," Jake observed. "Nothing is going to happen for hours. The house is just around the corner. Harry will stay here, just in case, and if anything looks like it's happening he'll call and we can be back in five minutes." He looked at Luke. "Frank and Elly are staying at the guest house. Have you got somewhere?"

"I never thought of it."

"Then you'd better come with us."

"Thanks, but I'm staying right here," he said firmly.

Frank put an arm about Josie. "Come along, darling," he said.

But Josie shook her head. "I want to stay with Daddy."

"It's very late and you ought to go to bed," Frank said firmly. "Come along now."

Josie's eyes filled with tears, and she looked at Luke, silently pleading.

Please, please Luke...don't fight over her.

He didn't know where the voice had come from. He could almost have sworn it was an external sound, but perhaps it had only echoed in his heart. Whatever the truth, it told him what he must do.

"On second thought, I'm going back to the guest house," he said. He turned to Frank and Elly. "Maybe we all need to be together."

It felt strange to be returning after all these years. The inside had been made over to look cheerful and modern, but basically it was the same place where he and Pippa had lived and loved, and lost each other.

Susan, Pippa's assistant, was in charge now. She frowned when she saw Luke. "I'm afraid it's full up."

"What about the room just down the corridor?" Luke asked.

"That's a storeroom."

"Can I see it?"

"But it's full of sheets and pillows," she insisted.

"I'd still like to see it."

He found himself counting the steps down the passage to the room that had once been his and Pippa's. There were exactly eight if you took large strides, or twelve if you took short running steps because you were trying to undress each other at the same time.

The room came as a shock. The walls were now lined with deep shelves on which were the house supplies, bedding, tins of food, detergent. The ironing board leaned against the wall, and a large sack of potatoes stood in a corner. Everywhere he looked he saw neatness and order.

"It's very—tidy." It was all he could think of to say.

"Ms. Davis is particular about tidiness," Susan assured him. "She says otherwise we'd never find anything."

"If I can have a few cushions and borrow some blankets, I'll sleep here."

"There's no need. You can have the sofa in the—"

"I'd rather be here," he said quietly.

Josie, who had slipped in after him, now darted away and returned with the sofa cushions, which she arranged on the floor. Then she took some blankets down and began to arrange them, too. From a cupboard she took a hanger, and indicated for Luke to give her his coat. Together they arranged it on the hanger, and he put it up on a peg.

"Susan's making something to eat," she said.

"I don't think I could—"

"I'll bring you some here, shall I?"

"Thanks," he said, gratefully. She'd known he wanted to be alone. Was that because of an instinctive understanding between him and his child, he wondered? Or because even she felt that he couldn't face things?

She brought him some food, and watched while he ate it. He had no appetite and would have left some, but she said, "Finish everything. You've got to keep your strength up," sounding like a wise little adult. He did so.

"Why did you want this room?" she asked.

He smiled and stroked a stray lock of hair away from her forehead. "Guess."

"You and Mommy?"

"Yes. We lived in here. We used to pay part of our rent by doing some of the cooking. That was the only way we could afford to live. We didn't have anything—but we had everything."

Then he broke completely, putting his head in his hands and sobbing without restraint. Pippa, who had made everything right, was no longer there, perhaps would never be there again. But there was someone else, someone who stretched small arms around him as far as they would go, and kissed him. He put his arms around her, and they clung together, saying nothing, because it was too terrible for words.

At last Elly came to put her to bed, but Josie set her chin. "I want to stay with Daddy," she said.

"Why doesn't Daddy come and put you to bed?" Elly suggested.

She agreed to this compromise, and they all went up to the room Josie and Elly were to share, with Frank in a box room across the corridor. The events of the past hours had left the little girl worn-out. Despite her fear for her mother she was half-asleep by the time she was ready for bed. She kissed Elly, but it was Luke's hand she clung to until she fell asleep. He gently disengaged his fingers and leaned down to kiss his sleeping child. When he looked up, he found Elly watching him kindly.

"Thank you," he said, and she nodded.

Back in the storeroom the night seemed to close in on him. Restlessly he began to rearrange his few items of furniture. He couldn't put the makeshift bed in the same place as the old one, because the shelves were in the way, but he managed to get it at the same angle. He didn't quite know why he'd done that, except that anything else seemed wrong.

He lay down and closed his eyes, and at once she was there, snuggling up against him, her tousled head on his shoulder, one arm about his neck. He opened his eyes again and sat up. Why had he returned to this room, where so much had once been his, so much that he'd thrown away? It was filled with Pippa, with her love, her joy, her passionate, selfless giving.

You're very good at holding off, aren't you Luke?

He got to his feet and switched the light on. The room seemed to mock him.

Just here had stood the table where he'd first fed her and been enchanted by her wacky nature. Over there had been the sofa with the creaking springs where she'd first kissed him and demolished all the defenses he'd thought he'd put up against her magic.

In that corner had stood the rickety chair that had collapsed beneath her, and she'd lain amid the ruins, laughing too much to move, until he'd pulled her up and into his arms, kissing her madly, adoring her because all life and warmth was in her, as though she'd found the secret of the world. But secretly afraid, too, because to love someone that much was like putting chains on your soul.

That's how you survive, isn't it? By never getting too close to anyone.

"No," he shouted. *"No!"*

But for all his denials, what they'd had back then had ended in this room where everything was neat, functional, dead. And it was his doing.

* * *

They were all there in the corridor again next morning, even the boarders who knew that they wouldn't be allowed into Pippa's room. They were her friends and they cared about her. Luke tried to think who would do the same for him. His family, of course, and Claudia, but not troops of unconnected people. Getting hundreds of hits on your Web site wasn't the same, somehow.

More waiting. More hours crawling by. The doctors had begun to lift the heavy sedation so that Pippa could regain consciousness. But she didn't, which, Luke could tell, worried them more than they wanted to admit.

Frank looked to be at the end of his tether. Luke regarded him with pity, feeling the old antagonism die. Josie made a movement toward him and Elly, but stopped, glancing quickly at Luke, as if torn between them. He touched her gently, whispering, "Go and talk to them." Watching her go, Luke found himself talking to Pippa in his head.

"You see? There'll be no tug-of-war on my side. That's what you wanted, isn't it? Where are you? Do you know?"

His life had contained little that could be called spiritual, but now he tried to believe that Pippa was there, watching him even while she slept in the next room. He *had* to believe that she knew.

More waiting. Why hadn't she come to? What weren't they telling him?

At last the door opened and the doctor beckoned, standing back for Luke and Josie to enter.

"She's beginning to move," he said.

They went quickly to either side of her bed. Pippa

was stirring, muttering inaudibly. The next moment she had opened her eyes, looking directly at Josie.

"Hallo, Mommy," the child said joyfully.

"Hallo, darling." She managed to move her arm a few inches in invitation, and Josie laid her head against it. Luke stood back, willing to wait for his moment.

At last it came. Josie said, "Mommy, look," pointing to him, and Pippa turned her head, just a little. Slowly he sank down until he was on his knees beside the bed so that she could see him more easily.

"Didn't you know I'd come, my love?" he asked.

She managed a faint smile. "I guess I did." Her eyes closed again.

"Pippa," he said urgently.

"She should rest now," the doctor said.

He let himself be shepherded out with Josie, but once outside he drew the doctor aside, speaking very quietly.

"How much does it really mean that she came around?"

"It helps," the doctor said after a pause, "but it's not conclusive."

"You're telling me that she could still die?"

"Yes, I am. It's good that she's regained consciousness, but some of the signs aren't as good as I'd hoped."

"I want to see her again, now. Just for a moment."

The doctor was about to make a formal protest, but something in Luke's eyes stopped him. "Two minutes," he said.

As he approached the bed again, he noticed how

poor Pippa's color was, almost the color of death. She was slipping away from him.

"Pippa," he said, "listen. I've got something important to ask you." He saw the question in her eyes. "It's this—will you marry me?"

"Ask me again," she whispered, "when I'm out of here."

"No, I mean now, today."

"Oh, yes—of course—Josie—"

"No," he said, becoming frantic with the need to make her understand. "You think I'm just trying to get a legal claim on her, but I'm not. It's not about her, it's about us. We should have been married years ago, and now, if—" he could hardly say it "—if I lose you, I want the world to know you were my wife. Not just my girlfriend, or the mother of my child, but my *wife*. Please, darling, marry me now. It would mean so much to me."

"Would it—really?"

"Everything in the world," he whispered.

"But can it be managed?"

"Leave everything to me. In the meantime—" From his pocket he took the engagement ring. "This is yours." He slid it gently onto her finger, and had the pleasure of seeing a glow come into her eyes.

"I didn't really want to give it back," she said.

"I'm going to fix everything. You—you be here when I get back, okay?"

"Okay. Luke—"

"Yes, darling?"

"Talk to Harry," she murmured. "He's studying law."

Luck was with him in one way because Harry was

right outside. But in another way it was against him, because Frank and Elly were there, too.

"If you think I'm going to allow this you're out of your mind," Frank said harshly. "I'm going to speak to the hospital authorities and have you thrown out. They won't let you pester a sick woman again—"

"Frank." Elly put a gentle hand on his arm. "It's no use. If this is what Pippa wants—how can we deny her, when it may be the last thing—"

Frank's shoulders shook. "Do as you please," he said hoarsely, and turned away.

Harry got to work on a special license, and because of the circumstances was able to get one within an hour. Then he went one better and produced an uncle who was a vicar.

Josie was sitting beside Pippa holding her hand when Luke returned.

"How is she?" he whispered.

"She keeps going to sleep and waking up again. Daddy, she says you're going to get married."

"We are."

Josie's face brightened. "When?"

"Today, just as soon as it can be fixed."

She beamed. "Can I be a bridesmaid?"

"Honey, it's going to happen right here, not in a church."

"But Mommy will still need a bridesmaid, because she's a bride."

"I guess she will."

Josie slipped out of the room, and Luke sat beside Pippa, taking her hand. Her eyes were closed. "You're going to be my wife," he said, "as you should have been all these years. When you're better we'll do it again with all the trimmings. You'll have the best wedding dress you can find, but you'll never look more beautiful to me than you do this minute.''

She opened her eyes and smiled sleepily, but he couldn't tell how much she'd heard.

One by one they came in, the friends from the guest house. Harry's vicar uncle slipped in timidly as though hoping not to be noticed. Frank and Elly were there, too, but standing apart, looking unhappy.

''Where's Josie?'' Elly asked.

''She vanished,'' Luke said, looking around in dismay.

But Josie returned at that moment, bearing two small bouquets. ''There's a flower shop down-stairs,'' she explained. ''Here, Mommy.'' She put the larger bouquet in her mother's hands as they lay weakly on the sheet.

''Thank you, darling.''

''Are we all ready?'' the vicar asked. ''If it's all right with you, I prefer to use the old-fashioned service.''

''Fine,'' Luke said. Then a horrible thought occurred to him. The old-fashioned service, which meant...

''Sir,'' he said in a loud whisper to the vicar, ''about this service—she won't obey.''

''I beg your pardon?''

''Cut out *obey*,'' Luke muttered urgently. ''She won't do it.''

''No, she flaming won't,'' Pippa murmured.

''Sorry about that,'' Luke said.

''No, no, I quite understand,'' the vicar said. ''They none of them do these days.''

The sigh that accompanied these words told volumes about the little vicar's domestic life. Luke's eyes met Pippa's and, incredibly, a spark of amusement flashed between them. She was close to death, but even now she couldn't resist sharing a joke with him. Luke closed his eyes for a moment, and a shudder went through him. She was so alive, it simply wasn't possible for her to die. It wasn't possible because he couldn't bear it.

Then he felt the weak movement against his hand and, looking down, saw that Pippa had reached out to him. He twined his fingers in hers and felt the comfort she was offering.

The vicar cleared his throat. "Dearly beloved, we are gathered together here…"

Luke didn't hear the next bit. He was watching Pippa's face, seeing her eyes fixed on him with a look of joyful wonder that smote him to the heart. In spite of everything, she loved him so much that this moment could make her happy.

The vicar inquired, "Who gives this woman to be married to this man?"

There was an awkward silence, because nobody had thought of it. Some of them looked at Harry, and some at Jake, but before either could speak, a voice from the back said, "I do."

Every head turned to see Frank come forward, pale but determined. "I do," he said again, taking Pippa's hand and offering it to Luke.

Pippa's eyes shone. "Thank you, Frank, dear."

Luke inclined his head to Frank in gratitude, knowing what the gesture would mean to Pippa. Then he realized that the vicar was asking if he would have this woman to be his wedded wife. He felt as if he was in another world as he made the response and listened as Pippa made hers.

Then came the moment Luke had dreaded, because he wasn't sure he could get through it without breaking down.

"I, Luke, take thee, Philippa, to be my wedded wife, to have and to hold...to love and to cherish, till death do us part...." His voice shook on the words, but her hand in his kept him safe.

Now it was Pippa's turn.

"I, Philippa, take thee, Luke, to be my wedded husband, to have and to hold...to love and to cherish, till death do us part."

When the vicar asked if he had the ring, Luke looked blank. In the agitation, he'd forgotten this part. But Elly was there, offering him her own ring. Then he was slipping it onto Pippa's finger. "With this ring, I thee wed..."

And she was his wife.

He looked down, hoping to meet her eyes, but Pippa had slipped into unconsciousness again.

"I want to stay with her all the time now," Luke told the doctor. "I won't disturb her, but I want to be with her."

"All right. Perhaps it'll do her some good, especially if you talk to her."

"Will she hear?"

"It's hard to tell, but we know that hearing is the last sense to go. There are cases of people in a deep coma who awoke and described everything they'd heard. It's not good that she's slipped back like this, and if you talk, it may make all the difference."

More waiting. Just himself and Josie now, one each side of the bed as the night passed. They took it in turns, one to talk, one to doze, trusting each other for what would happen if Pippa stirred. But the night wore wearily on, and still she didn't come back to them.

In the early hours he leaned over and kissed her while Josie did the same from the other side, but Pippa didn't react. That was the hardest thing, to make no impression on her at all, she who had been as swiftly responsive as quicksilver. It made him want to howl and bang his head against something to cover the fear and despair that were rising in him. But Josie was there, needing him to be strong, so he just smiled and squeezed his daughter's hand.

"Dad, it's like she doesn't know we're here."

"Of course she knows, honey. Remember what the doctor said. She can hear things, even when she's unconscious. Can't you, darling?" He gently brushed Pippa's face. "You know we're here, and you know what we're saying, especially when we say that we love you."

"But how does she know, Daddy?"

"I don't know. It's a mystery, just like love is a mystery. She knows how much we love her, and she can feel that love, wherever she is. And it's making her strong, so that she'll be able to find her way back to us."

"But where is she now?" Josie's eyes were on him, confident that he, too, was strong and wise and could take care of her.

"I'm not sure exactly where she is," he said carefully, "but it's a place where she needs to be until she's well enough to awaken."

"Like a sort of hospital inside?"

"Yes, just like that. She'll wake up when she's

ready, and she'll be better. Then we can look after her—you and I, you'll see—'' His voice broke.

"Yes, Daddy," Josie said softly, taking his hand.

More hours passed, but nobody was counting them now. Still Pippa lay motionless. Josie's head was on the bed. She wasn't crying openly, but her cheeks were wet, and Luke made a desperate decision.

"Josie," he said urgently, "she moved."

Her head came up. "What?"

"Your mother moved. I felt her squeeze my hand."

"Daddy—she's coming round?"

"Maybe not quite that," he said cautiously. "But she's closer."

"She's not squeezing my hand," Josie said anxiously.

"Be patient. She's there, darling. She's coming back to us."

They took a break to allow the others in. Luke went to stretch his legs and drink some coffee. When he returned, Josie slipped out and he had a precious moment alone with Pippa. Settling himself as close to her as he could get, so that his face was near hers, he murmured, "Darling, I told a terrible lie. I told Josie you squeezed my hand. She was thrilled. But it wasn't true. I didn't feel anything. I don't know if I did the right thing—maybe not—now she's longing for you to squeeze her hand, too, and what will she do if you don't? Please, darling, try. Try hard."

He hunted around for something new to say, but his mind was tired and it fixed on the coffee.

"I've just been drinking some really horrible

stuff, from a machine. Why don't the English learn to make coffee? When you're well, we'll teach them together. Then we'll leave for home. You're going to love living in Los Angeles. Josie, too. And think how the restaurants will flourish when the Greatest Cook in the World becomes my partner!

"I've got plans for us. We'll change the name to Luke & Pippa's Place, or Pippa & Luke's Place if you'd rather. Mind you, it's only a matter of time before one of them becomes Josie's Place. I expect she's planning it now. We'll do the show together, but I think we should restrict Josie to one show in six, otherwise the little scene-stealer will take over, and where will that leave us? Darling, it's going to be so marvelous, you and me together, for the rest of our lives. Whatever you want, that's what I want to give you. Always."

His throat was getting dry. He'd already talked so much without getting the feeling she was drawing any nearer to him.

"Please, darling," he begged. "Please."

Pictures and words began to run together in his exhausted mind. Their wedding, Frank giving her away, Elly lending him her ring, Elly reading Pippa's letter with its plea for peace between them for Josie's sake.

Luke sat up straight, calling himself a fool. Six words from the letter stood out in his head: *if it should come to that...* She'd meant, if she should die.

Pippa hadn't been thinking of what would become of her, but beyond that to the welfare of the one who most needed her protection. Not himself, but

Josie. Everything she'd done had been for Josie. Even, perhaps, marrying him. And she was right.

Now she cared about only one thing, to know that her child would be safe when she was no longer there. Then she could be at peace.

He'd told her how much he longed to give her, but all she wanted was this: to die in peace.

"No!" he said with soft vehemence. "Ask me anything else."

But she had nothing else to ask him.

Whatever you want, that's what I want to give you. His own words seemed to mock him. How easy they had been to say, before he knew the price that would be asked.

"If you—if I—if we lose each other," he began haltingly, and stopped. He didn't know how to go on. But suddenly the words came. "I won't ever let you down again. Josie will have a real father, I promise. A good father. As good as I know how to be.

"Fine words, right? And you're thinking, does this idiot really know what he's promising? Of course I don't. But I'll pick it up day by day, with Josie to help me. And you'll help me, too, because I'll have all my memories of you. If I try to raise her to be half the woman her mother is, I won't go far wrong. Neither of us will ever forget you, and I'll never stop loving you, as long as I live."

He looked down at her lying on the pillow and bent to kiss her softly.

"Goodbye, my darling," he whispered.

Josie slipped inside the room. "Has it happened yet, Daddy?" she asked urgently. "Has she squeezed your hand again?"

Dismayed, he realized that he'd forgotten his rash promise. Josie took one of her mother's hands in hers. "Mommy," she appealed, "Daddy said you were coming back."

"Josie," Luke reached for her, "there's something—"

"Daddy!" Josie's shriek was deafening.

"What is it?"

"She did it. She squeezed my hand."

And in the same moment he felt the pressure of Pippa's fingers on his, incredibly strong, like someone who'd been saving her strength for this moment.

"Daddy, look. Her eyes are opening."

"Pippa? *Pippa!*"

"Hello, Luke. You really were there, all the time?"

"All the time," he said huskily.

He stood back to leave mother and daughter alone. Besides, he needed to be unobserved for a moment, because suddenly his eyes were blurred and his throat ached. Josie hurried out to spread the good news, and he went to kneel by Pippa again.

"I heard you," she whispered.

"Then you know how much I love you, Pippa."

She smiled. "I always wondered."

"How much did you actually hear?"

"A lot, especially at the end."

"I didn't want you to leave, but I thought maybe you had no choice."

"I thought I didn't. But then I heard you, and I knew I couldn't bear to leave you. I never thought you'd make it easy for me."

"I told you I'd do anything you wanted. I was even going to promise to let Frank and Elly be a part of her life. They could teach her all the sensible things I don't know about, at least until I've had a chance to learn them. But I'd much rather you taught me."

Her lips twitched. "I wouldn't dream of it. One of us being sensible is enough. Never change, my darling."

"Never," he promised. "For the rest of our lives."

"For the rest of our lives."

Josie stood at one of the plate-glass windows at LAX airport, staring at the planes basking in the April sun. She was frowning as though the sight displeased her, which it did. For despite the bustle of activity there was no sign of the plane she wanted.

"I hate it when things are late," she said fretfully.

"Only half an hour, darling," Pippa said, laughing at her daughter's disgusted face.

"But Uncle Frank, Aunt Elly and Sam are only going to be here two weeks, and we've lost half an hour."

"Don't worry, it'll probably be late leaving, too," Luke soothed her. "So it'll work out even."

"I'm going to find out," Josie said. "No, you stay here, Mom. You shouldn't walk any more than you have to."

"Darling, I'm only four months gone. It's not for ages yet."

"Josie's right," Luke said. "We'll all stay here. There'll be another announcement soon."

"Mom, if it's a boy, can we call him George?"

"You want to call your brother after a dog?" Luke demanded.

"He was a nice dog," Josie said defiantly.

"Just the same—"

"Will you two hush?" Pippa said. "I don't want to hear this argument again until he or she is born."

"He," Luke said firmly. "I want a boy."

"You're a male chauvinist whatsit!" Josie informed him.

"No, I'm not," he defended himself. "It's just that I've already got one daughter, and my nerves couldn't stand another." But he kissed the top of her head as he said it.

"I wonder what Sam's like," Josie mused.

"I only know what Elly told me," Pippa told her. "He's eleven years old, they've been fostering him since Christmas, and it's working out very well. Apparently he's quiet and a bit shy, but Elly thinks you'll soon change all that."

"You bet!" Josie confirmed. "I'm going to see what's happening." She bounded away.

Pippa turned to say something to her husband and found him brooding. It was unlike him, and had happened once or twice before, she realized.

"What is it, darling? Worried about the restaurants?"

"Nope. Profits are up. Your Siberian cherries are a big hit. Yesterday somebody congratulated me on my 'brilliant creation.' I came that close to taking the credit."

She chuckled. She believed him.

"And Ritchie's over the moon at the impact you made on the TV program," Luke added.

"So what is it?"

"Just a passing thought."

"A thought? You?" she teased. "Best let it pass, then. You wouldn't know what to do with it."

"You're so clever, Mrs. Danton. Funny how good that sounds. 'Mrs.' It used to sound like a padlock. Now I don't care if they lock the door and throw away the key, as long as I'm on the inside with you and Josie and George."

"So what's on your mind?"

"Just that I wonder how it happened. Or rather why. I've sometimes had this strange feeling that you only married me for Josie's sake."

"Really? Well, it probably does you a lot of good to wonder."

"I thought you'd say that. You might even be right. Keep him on his toes. Let him worry that he's only second best."

"You're forgetting George."

"Third best." He waited for her to deny it.

"Darling," she chuckled, "you really must get out of this habit of thinking joined-up thoughts. You're not used to it, and it's scrambling your brains."

"So?"

"So who says you're third best?"

"Well, you haven't said I'm not," he told her.

"Maybe that's because I can't get a word in edge-wise."

He looked at her. She looked at him.

"You aren't going to tell me, are you?"

Pippa kissed him tenderly, and smiled.

"Probably not," she said.

*   *   *   *   *

That's My Baby!

**Don't miss these
heartwarming stories
coming to THAT'S MY BABY—
only from Silhouette Special Edition.**

August 2000:

WHEN BABY WAS BORN
by **Jodi O'Donnell** (SE #1339)

Sara was about to give birth—and couldn't remember
anything except her name! But then a twist of fate brought
dashing cowboy Cade McGivern to the rescue....

October 2000:

BACHELOR'S BABY PROMISE
by **Barbara McMahon** (SE #1351)

Jared Montgomery wasn't looking for love—until the
handsome new father fell for the blue-eyed beauty
who tenderly cared for his adorable baby girl.

**THAT'S MY BABY!
Sometimes bringing up baby can
bring surprises...and showers of love!**

Available at your favorite retail outlet.

Silhouette®
Where love comes alive™

Visit Silhouette at www.eHarlequin.com   SSETMB00

Through the darkness,
love illuminates the way home....

GINNA GRAY

THE
PRODIGAL
Daughter

Seven years ago
Maggie Malone lost
everything one hellish night
and left Ruby Falls, Texas, in
disgrace. Now Maggie has
come home.

Her father is dying
and so is their proud
family business. Maggie had once dreamed of
running the empire—and old dreams die hard. But
to claim them, she'll have to confront the father
who denies her, the family who resents her, the
secrets that surround her, the man who wants
her...and the treachery closing in on them all.

Ginna Gray "is one of the most consistently
excellent writers in the genre today."
—*Romantic Times*

*On sale September 2000
wherever paperbacks are sold!*

**Don't miss
an exciting opportunity
to save on the purchase of
Harlequin and Silhouette books!**

Buy any two Harlequin or
Silhouette books and save
$10.00 off future Harlequin
and Silhouette purchases

OR

buy any three
Harlequin or Silhouette books
and save **$20.00 off** future
Harlequin and Silhouette purchases.

*Watch for details
coming in October 2000!*

PHQ400

where love comes alive—online...

Visit the *Author's Alcove*

➢ Find the most complete information anywhere on
your favorite Silhouette author.

➢ Try your hand in the Writing Round Robin—
contribute a chapter to an online book in the
making.

Enter the *Reading Room*

➢ Experience an interactive novel—help determine
the fate of a story being created now by one of
your favorite authors.

➢ Join one of our reading groups and discuss your
favorite book.

Drop into *Shop eHarlequin*

➢ Find the latest releases—read an excerpt or write
a review for this month's Silhouette top sellers.

➢ Try out our amazing search feature—tell us your
favorite theme, setting or time period and we'll find
a book that's perfect for you.

All this and more available at

www.eHarlequin.com
on Women.com Networks

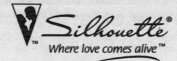

COMING NEXT MONTH

#1351 BACHELOR'S BABY PROMISE—Barbara McMahon
That's My Baby!
Jared Montgomery wasn't looking for love—until the tall, dark and handsome geologist fell for the blue-eyed beauty he hired to watch his baby girl. Could the winsome ways of nurturing schoolteacher Jenny Stratford transform this most stubborn of bachelors?

#1352 MARRYING A DELACOURT—Sherryl Woods
And Baby Makes Three: The Delacourts of Texas
Strong-willed Grace Foster had left the dashing but difficult Michael Delacourt when she'd realized he was married to his job. Now, to win her back, he was going to have to prove that love was his most important mission of all.

#1353 MILLIONAIRE TAKES A BRIDE—Pamela Toth
Here Come the Brides
When charming rogue Ryan Noble set his mind on taking a bride, he did just that. Trouble was, he claimed Sarah Daniels…the wrong twin! To make matters worse, his *un*intended bride's irresistible allure was stealing *his* heart.

#1354 A BUNDLE OF MIRACLES—Amy Frazier
Rugged police chief Ben Chase built an impenetrable exterior after his beloved Abbie Latham left town without explanation. Only a miracle could reunite these two soul mates separated by a painful secret. Was the bundled-up baby on Abbie's doorstep the sign they'd been waiting for?

#1355 HIDDEN IN A HEARTBEAT—Patricia McLinn
A Place Called Home
Primly proper Rebecca Dahlgren came to Wyoming to learn about her Native American heritage—not to fall for some irksome cattle rancher. But Luke Chandler's powerful presence and passionate kisses were arousing desires she couldn't ignore!

#1356 STRANGER IN A SMALL TOWN—Ann Roth
Single mom Alison O'Hara was struggling to make ends meet when brooding stranger Clint Strong became her new tenant. A few fiery embraces stirred up feelings she'd forgotten existed. But while Alison might have opened the door to her home, would she welome him into her heart?

CMN0900